REPLICA
LYRA

AUTHOR'S NOTE

Although in many cases you will find identical portions of dialogue occurring from both Gemma's and Lyra's perspectives in their respective narratives, you may also notice minor variations in tone and tempo. This was done deliberately to reflect their individual perspectives. Gemma and Lyra have unique conceptual frameworks that actively interact with and thus define their experiences, just as the act of observing a thing immediately alters the behavior of the thing itself.

The minor variations in the novel reflect the belief that there is no single objective experience of the world. No one sees or hears the same thing in exactly the same way, as anyone who has ever been in an argument with a loved one can attest. In that way we truly are inventors of our own experience. The truth, it turns out, looks a lot like making fiction.

LAUREN OLIVER

REPLICA

LYRA

HODDER &
STOUGHTON

First published in the US in 2016 by HarperCollins Children's Books
A division of HarperCollins Publishers

First published in Great Britain in 2016 by Hodder & Stoughton
An Hachette UK company

1

A CIP catalogue record for this title is available from the British Library

. Hardback ISBN 978 1 473 61495 6
Trade Paperback ISBN 978 1 473 61496 3
Ebook ISBN 978 1 473 61497 0

Printed and bound by Clays Ltd, St Ives plc

Hodder & Stoughton policy is to use papers that are natural,
renewable and recyclable products and made from wood grown in sustainable
forests. The logging and manufacturing processes are expected to conform
to the environmental regulations of the country of origin.

Hodder & Stoughton Ltd
Carmelite House
50 Victoria Embankment
London EC4Y 0DZ

www.hodder.co.uk

To my sister, Lizzie

ONE

ON VERY STILL NIGHTS SOMETIMES we can hear them chanting, calling for us to die. We can see them, too, or at least make out the halo of light cast up from the shores of Barrel Key, where they must be gathered, staring back across the black expanse of water toward the fence and the angular white face of the Haven Institute. From that distance it must look like a long green jaw set with miniature teeth.

Monsters, they call us. Demons.

Sometimes, on sleepless nights, we wonder if they're right.

Lyra woke up in the middle of the night with the feeling that someone was sitting on her chest. Then she realized it was just the heat – swampy and thick, like the pressure of somebody's hand. The power had gone down.

Something was wrong. People were shouting. Doors slammed. Footsteps echoed in the halls. Through the windows, she saw the zigzag pattern of flashlights cutting across the courtyard, illuminating silvery specks of rain and the stark-white statue of a man, reaching down toward the ground, as though to pluck something from the earth. The other replicas came awake simultaneously. The dorm was suddenly full of voices, thick with sleep. At night it was easier to speak. There were fewer nurses to shush them.

'What's wrong?'

'What's happened?'

'Be quiet.' That was Cassiopeia. 'I'm listening.'

The door from the hall swung open, so hard it cracked against the wall. Lyra was dazzled by a sudden sweep of light.

'They all here?' It sounded like Dr. Coffee Breath.

'I think so.' Nurse Don't-Even-Think-About-It's voice was high and terrified. Her face was invisible behind the flashlight beam. Lyra could make out just the long hem of her nightgown and her bare feet.

'Well, count them.'

'We're all here,' Cassiopeia responded. One of them gasped. But Cassiopeia was never afraid to speak up. 'What's going on?'

'It must be one of the males,' Dr. Coffee Breath said

to Nurse Don't-Even-Think-About-It, who was really named Maxine. 'Who's checking the males?'

'What's wrong?' Cassiopeia repeated. Lyra found herself touching the windowsill, the pillow, the headboard of bed number 24. Her things. Her world.

At that moment, the answer came to them: voices, shrill, calling to one another. *Code Black. Code Black. Code Black.*

Almost at the same time, the backup generator kicked on. The lights came up, and with them, the alarms. Sirens wailed. Lights flashed in every room. Everyone squinted in the sudden brightness. Nurse Don't-Even-Think-About-It stumbled backward, raising an arm as though to shield herself from view.

'Stay here,' Dr. Coffee Breath said. Lyra wasn't sure whether he was speaking to Nurse Don't-Even-Think-About-It or to the replicas. Either way, there wasn't much choice. Dr. Coffee Breath had to let himself into the hall with a code. Nurse Don't-Even-Think-About-It stayed for only a moment, shivering, her back to the door, as if she expected that at any second the girls might make a rush at her. Her flashlight, now subsumed by the overheads, cast a milk-white ring on the tile floor.

'Ungrateful,' she said, before she, too, let herself out. Even then they could see her through the windows overlooking the hall, moving back and forth, occasionally touching her cross.

'What's Code Black?' Rose asked, hugging her knees to her chest. They'd run out of stars ever since Dr. O'Donnell, the only staff member Lyra had never nick-named, had stopped giving them lessons. Instead the replicas selected names for themselves from the collection of words they knew, words that struck them as pretty or interesting. There was Rose, Palmolive, and Private. Lilac Springs and Tide. There was even a Fork.

As usual, only Cassiopeia – number 6, one of the oldest replicas besides Lyra – knew.

'Code Black means security's down,' she said. 'Code Black means someone's escaped.'

TWO

H-U-M-A-N. THE FIRST WORD WAS *hu-man*.

There were two kinds of humans: natural-born humans, people, women and men, girls and boys, like the doctors and staff, the researchers, the guards, and the Suits who came sometimes to survey the island and its inhabitants.

Then there were human models, males and females, made in the laboratory and transferred to the surrogate birthers, who lived in the barracks and never spoke English. The *clones*, people occasionally still called them, though Lyra knew this was a bad word, a hurtful word, even though she didn't know why. At Haven they were called replicas.

The second word was *M-O-D-E-L*. She spelled it, breathing the sounds lightly between her teeth, the way that Dr. O'Donnell had taught her. Then: the number 24.

So the report *was* about her.

'How are you feeling today?' Nurse Swineherd asked. Lyra had named her only last month. She didn't know what a swineherd was but had heard Nurse Rachel say, *Some days I'd rather be a swineherd*, and had liked the sound of it. 'Lots of excitement last night, huh?' As always, she didn't wait for a response, and instead forced Lyra down onto the examination table, so she no longer had a view of the file.

Lyra felt a quick flash of anger, like a temporary burst in her brain. It wasn't that she was curious about the report. She had no desire in particular to know about herself, to find out why she was sick and whether she could be cured. She understood, in general terms, from things insinuated or overheard, that there were still glitches in the process. The replicas were born genetically identical to the source material but soon presented with various medical problems, organs that didn't function properly, blood cells that didn't regenerate, lungs that collapsed. As they got older, they lost their balance, forgot words and place names, became easily confused, and cried more. Or they simply *failed to thrive* in the first place. They stayed skinny and stunted. They smashed their heads on the floor, and when the Suits came, screamed to be picked up. (In the past few years God had mandated that the newest generational crops be picked up, bounced, or engaged in play for at least two hours every day. Research suggested that human contact would keep them healthier for longer. Lyra and the other older replicas took turns with them, tickling their fat little feet, trying to make them smile.)

Lyra had fallen in love with reading during the brief, ecstatic period of time when Dr. O'Donnell had been at Haven, which she now thought of as the best months of her life. When Lyra read, it was as if a series of small windows opened in the back of her mind, flooding her with light and fresh air and visions of other places, other lives, *other*, period. The only books at Haven were books about science and the body, and these were difficult and full of words she couldn't sound out. But she read charts when they were left unattended on countertops. She read the magazines the nurses left behind in their break room.

Nurse Swineherd kept talking while she took Lyra's blood pressure with Squeezeme and stuck Thermoscan under her tongue. Lyra liked Squeezeme and Thermoscan. She liked the way Squeezeme tightened around her upper arm, like a hand holding on to lead her somewhere. She liked Thermoscan's reassuring beeps, and afterward when Nurse Swineherd said, 'Perfectly normal.'

She added, 'Don't know what it was thinking, running that way. Breathe deeply, okay? Good. Now exhale. Good. It'll drown before it gets past the breaks. Did you hear the surf last night? Like thunder! I'm surprised the body hasn't turned up already, actually.'

Lyra knew she wasn't expected to reply. The one time she had, in response to Nurse Swineherd's cheerful question, 'How are we today?' Nurse Swineherd had startled, dropping one of the syringes – Lyra hated the syringes, refused to name them – and had to start over. But she wondered what it would be like to come across the dead body on the beach. She wasn't afraid of dead bodies. She had seen hundreds of replicas get sick and die. All the Yellows had died, none of them older than twelve months. *A fluke*, the doctors said: *a fever*. Lyra had seen the bodies wrapped and prepared for shipping.

A Purple from the seventh crop, number 333, had simply stopped eating. By the time they put her on a tube, it was too late. Number 501 swallowed twenty-four small white Sleepers after Nurse Em, who used to help shave her head and was always gentlest with the razor, went away. Number 421 had gone suddenly, in her sleep. It was Lyra who'd touched her arm to wake her and known, from the strange plastic coldness of her body, that she was dead. Strange that in an instant all the life just evaporated, went away, leaving only the skin and bones, a pile of flesh.

But that's what they were: bodies. Human and yet not people. She hadn't so far been able to figure out why. She looked, she thought, like a normal person. So did the other female replicas. They'd been *made* from normal people, and even birthed from them.

But the making of them marked them. That's what everybody said. Except for Dr. O'Donnell.

She wouldn't mind seeing a male up close – the male and female replicas were kept separate, even the dead ones that went off the island in tarps. She was curious about the males, had studied the anatomical charts in the medical textbooks she couldn't otherwise read. She had looked especially closely at diagrams of the female and male reproductive organs, which seemed, she thought, to mark the primary difference between them, but she couldn't imagine what a male's would look like in real life. The only men she saw were doctors, nurses, security, and other members of the staff.

'All right. Almost done. Come here and stand on the scale now, okay?'

Lyra stood up, hoping to catch a glimpse once again of the chart, and its beautiful, symmetrical lettering, which marched like soldiers across the page. But Nurse Swineherd had snatched the clipboard and was writing in Lyra's newest results. Without releasing her grip on the clipboard, she adjusted the scale expertly with one hand, waiting until it balanced correctly.

'Hmmm.' She frowned, so that the lines between her eyebrows deepened and converged. Once, when Lyra was really little, she had announced that she had found out the difference between people and replicas: people were old, replicas were young. The nurse who was bathing her at the time, a nurse who hadn't stayed long, and whose name Lyra could no longer remember, had burst out laughing. The story had quickly made the rounds among the nurses and doctors.

'You've lost weight,' Nurse Swineherd said, still frowning. 'How's your appetite?'

Several seconds went by before Lyra realized this was a question she was meant to answer. 'Fine.'

'No nausea? Cramping? Vomiting?'

Lyra shook her head.

'Vision problems? Confusion?'

Lyra shook her head because she wasn't very practiced at lying. Two weeks ago she'd vomited so intensely her ribs had ached the following day. Yesterday she'd thrown up in a pillowcase, hoping it would help muffle the sound. Fortunately she'd been able to sneak it in with the rest of the trash, which went off on boats on Sundays, to be burned or dumped into the sea or otherwise disposed of. Given the storm, and the security breach, and the now-probably-dead male, she was confident no one would notice the missing pillowcase.

But the worst thing was that she had gotten lost yesterday, on her way back to the dorms. It didn't make any sense. She knew every inch of D-Wing, from Natal

Intensive to Neural Observation, to the cavernous dorms that housed one hundred female replicas each, to the bathrooms with dozens of showerheads tacked to a wall, a trench-like sink, and ten toilets. But she must have turned right instead of left coming out of the bathroom and had somehow ended up at the locked door that led into C-Wing, blinking confusedly, until a guard had called out to her and startled her into awareness.

But she wouldn't say so. She couldn't go to the Box. That's what everyone called G-Wing. The Box, or the Funeral Home, because half the replicas that went in never came out.

'All right, off you go,' Nurse Swineherd said. 'You let me know if you start feeling sick, okay?'

This time, she knew she wasn't expected to answer. She wouldn't have to tell anyone she kept throwing up. That was what the Glass Eyes mounted in the ceiling were for. (She wasn't sure whether she liked the Glass Eyes or not. Sometimes she did, when the chanting from Barrel Key was especially loud and she thought the cameras were keeping her safe. Sometimes, when she wanted to hide that she felt sick, she hated them, those lashless lenses recording her every move. That was the problem: she never knew which side the Glass Eyes were on.)

But she nodded anyway. Lyra had a plan, and the plan required her to be good, at least for a little while.

THREE

THREE DAYS LATER, THE BODY of male number 72 had still not washed up on the beach, as everyone had predicted. At breakfast the day after trash day, Lyra heard the nurses discussing it. Don't-Even-Think-About-It shook her head and said she was sure the gators had gotten him. If he did make it onto the mainland, she said, he'd likely be shot on sight – nothing but crazies and criminals living out here for miles. *And now those men are coming,* she added, shaking her head. That was what all the nurses called the Suits: *those men.*

Lyra had seen their boat in the distance on her way into breakfast: a sleek, motorized schooner, so unlike the battered barge that carted supplies in and trash out and looked as if it was one teaspoon of water away from sinking. She didn't know exactly what the Suits did, who they were, or why they visited Haven. Over the years she'd heard several references to the military, although they didn't look like soldiers, at least not the ones she occasionally saw on the nurses' TV. These men didn't wear matching outfits, or pants covered in camouflage. They didn't carry weapons, like the guards did.

When she was younger, the Suits had made Lyra nervous, particularly when all the replicas were forced to line up in front of them to be inspected. The Suits had opened her mouth to look at her teeth. They had asked her to smile or turn around or clap on command, to show she wasn't an idiot, wasn't *failing to thrive*, to wiggle her fingers or move her eyes from left to right.

The inspections had stopped a long time ago, however. Now the Suits came, walked through all the wings, from Admin to the Box, spoke to God, and then returned to the mainland on their boat, and Lyra found that she'd grown less and less interested in them. They belonged to another world. They might as well have been flies touching down, only to take flight again. They didn't matter to her, not like Thermoscan did, not like her little bed and her windowsill and the meaning embedded deep in a hieroglyph of words.

Today, in particular, she couldn't think about the Suits, or the mysterious disappearance of number 72. The day after trash day was Monday, which meant Cog Testing, and Lazy Ass, and her last opportunity for a week.

Lyra couldn't remember when the idea of stealing from Admin had first come to her. It had started, in a way, with Dr. O'Donnell. Dr. O'Donnell had come to Haven six or seven years ago; it was before Lyra had her monthly bleeding. ('Your period,' Don't-Even-Think-About-It had said gruffly, and, in a rare moment of generosity, shown Lyra how to scrub out her underwear with cold water. 'Bleeding makes it sound like a gunshot wound.') Dr. O'Donnell was – apart from Cassiopeia and numbers 7–10, her four genotypes, all of them genetically and physically identical – the prettiest person at Haven.

Unlike the other nurses and doctors, Dr. O'Donnell didn't seem to dislike the replicas. She hung around in the dorms even when she wasn't assigned to monitor. She asked questions. She was the first person who'd ever asked Lyra a question and actually expected a reply – other than 'Does it hurt when I touch you there?' or 'How's your appetite?' – and laughed easily, especially over the things the replicas believed, like that the rest of the world must be the size of five or six Havens or that in natural-born humans fathers served no purpose. She taught the replicas clapping games and sang to them in a high, clear voice.

Dr. O'Donnell was shocked when she found out that Haven had no library – only medical textbooks occasionally used for reference moldering in an awkwardly shaped room no one quite knew the use for, and the Bible that

Don't-Even-Think-About-It carted around with her, and occasionally used to take a swipe at replicas that disobeyed her, or to whack the ones too idiotic and brain-scrambled to follow instructions at all.

Whenever Dr. O'Donnell left the island, she returned with a few books in her bag. On Sunday afternoons, she sat in the dorms and read out loud. First it was only books with lots of pictures. Then longer books, with small type running across every page, so many letters it made Lyra dizzy to look. A few dozen replicas always gathered around to hear the stories, and afterward, after lights-out, repeated them in whispers for the other replicas, often making up or mixing up details, Jack and the Bean-stalk that grew to Oz; the Lion, the Witch, and the Big Friendly Giant. It was a relief from the boredom, from the smallness of the world. Five wings, six counting the Box. Half the doors locked. All the world circumscribed by water. Half the replicas too dumb to talk, another quarter of them too sick, and still more too angry and violent.

No escape. Never escape.

But for Lyra, something deeper happened. She fell in love, although she didn't know it and would never have thought in those terms, since she didn't understand what love was and had only rarely heard the word. Under the influence of Dr. O'Donnell's voice, and her long fingers (some of them scattered with tiny freckles) turning the pages, a long-buried part of her consciousness woke, stirred, and opened.

Dr. O'Donnell was the one who had taught them the names for the various constellations – Hercules and Lyra, Cassiopeia and Venus, Ursa Major and Minor – and explained that stars were masses made of white-hot gas, hundreds upon hundreds upon hundreds of miles, farther than they could imagine.

Lyra remembered sitting on her cot one Sunday afternoon, while Dr. O'Donnell read to them from one of Lyra's favorite books, *Goodnight Moon*, and suddenly Cassiopeia – who was known only as 6 then – spoke up.

'I want a name,' she'd said. 'I want a name like the stars have.'

And Lyra had felt profoundly embarrassed: she'd thought 6 was Cassiopeia's name, just as 24 was hers.

Dr. O'Donnell had gone around the room, assigning names. 'Cassiopeia,' she said. 'Ursa. Venus. Calliope.' Calliope, formerly 7 and the meanest of Cassiopeia's genotypes, giggled. Dr. O'Donnell's eyes clicked to Lyra's. 'Lyra,' she said, and Lyra felt a little electrical jolt, as if she'd just touched something too hot.

Afterward she went through Haven naming things, marking them as familiar, as hers. Everyone called G-Wing the Box, but she named other places too, named the mess hall Stew Pot, and C-Wing, where the male replicas were kept, the Hidden Valley. The security cameras that tracked her everywhere were Glass Eyes, the blood pressure monitor wrapped around her upper arm Squeezeme. All the nurses got names, and the doctors too, at least the ones she saw regularly. She couldn't name the researchers or the birthers because she hardly ever saw them, but the barracks where the birthers slept she named the Factory, since that's where all the new human models came out, before they were transferred to Postnatal and then, if they survived, to the dorms, to be bounced and tickled and engaged at least two hours a day.

She named Dr. Saperstein God, because he controlled everything.

Lyra was always careful to sit next to Dr. O'Donnell when she read, with her head practically in Dr. O'Donnell's lap, to try to make sense of the dizzying swarm of brushstroke symbols as Dr. O'Donnell read, to try to tack the sounds down to the letters. She concentrated so hard, it made the space behind her eyeballs ache.

One day, it seemed to her that Dr. O'Donnell began reading more slowly – not so slowly that the others would notice, but just enough that Lyra could make better sense of the edges of the words and how they snagged on the edges of certain letters, before leaping over the little white spaces of the page. At first she thought it was her imagination. Then, when Dr. O'Donnell placed a finger on the page, and began tracing individual lines of text, tapping occasionally the mysterious dots and dashes, or pausing underneath a particularly entangled word, Lyra knew that it wasn't.

Dr. O'Donnell was trying to help Lyra to read.

And slowly, slowly – like a microscope adjusted by degrees and degrees, ticking toward clearer resolution – words began to free themselves from the mysterious inky puddles on the page, to throw themselves suddenly at Lyra's understanding. *I. And. Went. Now.*

It couldn't last. Lyra should have known, but of course she didn't.

She had just gotten a name. She'd been born, really, for the second time. She hardly knew anything.

One Sunday afternoon, Dr. O'Donnell didn't come. The girls waited for nearly an hour before Cassiopeia, growing bored, announced she was going to walk down to the beach behind A-Wing and try to collect seashells. Although it wasn't strictly forbidden, Cassiopeia was one of the few replicas that ever ventured down to the water. Lyra had sometimes followed her, but was too scared to go on her own – frightened of the stories the nurses told, of man-eating sharks in Wahlee Sound, of alligators and poisonous snakes in the marshes.

It was a pretty day, not too hot, and great big clouds puffed up with importance. But Lyra didn't want to go outside. She didn't want to do anything but sit on the floor next to Dr. O'Donnell, so close she could smell the mix of antiseptic and lemon lotion on her skin, and the fibers of the paper puffing into the air whenever Dr. O'Donnell turned the page.

She had a terrible thought: Dr. O'Donnell must be sick. It was the only explanation. She had never missed a Sunday since the readings had begun, and Lyra refused to believe that Dr. O'Donnell had simply grown tired of their Sunday afternoons together. That *she* was tiring. That she was too damaged, too slow for Dr. O'Donnell.

Forgetting that she hated the Box, that she held her breath whenever she came within fifty feet of its red-barred doors, Lyra began to run in that direction. She couldn't explain the sudden terror that gripped her, a feeling like waking in the middle of the night, surrounded by darkness, and having no idea where she was.

She'd nearly reached C-Wing when she heard the sudden rise of angry voices – one of them Dr. O'Donnell's. She drew back, quickly, into an alcove. She could just make out Dr. O'Donnell and God, facing off in one of the empty testing rooms. The door was partially open, and their voices floated out into the hall.

'I hired you,' God said, 'to do your job, not to play at Mother goddamn Teresa.' He raised his hand, and Lyra thought he might hit her. Then she saw that he was holding the old, weathered copy of *The Little Prince* Dr. O'Donnell had been reading.

'Don't you see?' Dr. O'Donnell's face was flushed. Her freckles had disappeared. 'What we're doing . . . Christ. They deserve a little happiness, don't they? Besides, you said yourself they do better when they get some affection.'

'Stimulation and touch. Not weekly story time.' God slammed the book down on a table, and Lyra jumped. Then he sighed. 'We're not humanitarians. We're *scientists*, Cat. And they're subjects. End of story.'

Dr. O'Donnell raised her chin. Her hair was starting to come loose from her ponytail. If Lyra had known the word *love*, if she'd really understood it, she would have known she loved Dr. O'Donnell in that moment.

'That doesn't mean we can't treat them like regular people,' she said.

God had already started for the door. Lyra caught a glimpse of his heavy black eyebrows, his close-trimmed beard, his eyes so sunken it looked like someone had pressed them back into his head. Now he stiffened and spun around. 'Actually, it does,' he said. His voice was very cold, like the touch of the Steel Ear when it slipped beneath her shirt to listen to her heartbeat. 'What's next? Are you going to start teaching the rats to play chess?'

Before she left Haven, Dr. O'Donnell gave Lyra her copy of *The Little Prince*. Then Lyra was pretty sure Dr. O'Donnell had been crying.

'Be sure and keep it hidden,' she whispered, and briefly touched Lyra's face.

Afterward, Lyra lay down. And for the afternoon, Lyra's pillow smelled like antiseptic and lemon lotion, like Dr. O'Donnell's fingers.

FOUR

COG TESTING TOOK PLACE IN a large, drafty room of D-Wing that had once been used to house cages full of rabbits and still smelled faintly of pellet food and animal urine. Lyra didn't know what had happened to the rabbits. Haven was large, and many of its rooms were off-limits, so she assumed they had been moved. Or maybe they had *failed to thrive,* too, like so many of the replicas.

Every week Cog Testing varied: the replicas might be asked to pick up small and slippery pins as quickly as possible, or attempt to assemble a three-dimensional puzzle, or to pick out visual patterns on a piece of paper. The female replicas, all nine hundred and sixty of them, were admitted by color in groups of forty over the course of the day. Lilac Springs was out of the Box and took the seat next to Lyra's. Lilac Springs had named herself after a product she'd seen advertised on the nurses' TV. Even after the nurses had laughed hysterically and explained to her – and everyone – what a feminine douche was and what it was for, she had refused to change her name, saying she liked the sound of it.

'You don't look so good' was the first thing Lilac Springs said to Lyra. Lilac Springs hardly ever said anything. She was one of the slower replicas. She still needed help getting dressed, and she had never learned her alphabet. 'Are you sick?'

Lyra shook her head, keeping her eyes on the table. She'd thrown up again in the middle of the night and was so dizzy afterward that she had to stay there, holding onto the toilet, for a good twenty minutes. Cassiopeia had caught her when she came in to pee. But she didn't think Cassiopeia would tell. Cassiopeia was always getting in trouble – for not eating her dinner, for talking, for openly staring at the males and even for trying to talk to them, on the few occasions they wound up in the halls or the Box or the Stew Pot together.

'*I'm* sick,' Lilac Springs said. She was speaking so loudly, Lyra instinctively looked up at the Glass Eyes, even though she knew they didn't register sound. 'They put me in the Box.'

Lyra didn't have friends at Haven. She didn't know what a friend was. But she thought she would be unhappy if Lilac Springs died. Lyra had been five years old when

Lilac Springs was made, and could still remember how after Lilac Springs had been birthed and transferred to Postnatal for observation she had kicked her small pink feet and waved her fists as if she was dancing.

But it wasn't looking good. Something was going around the Browns, and the doctors in the Box couldn't stop it. In the past four months, five of them had died – four females, and number 312 from the males' side. Two of them had died the same night. The nurses had suited up in heavy gloves and masks and bundled the bodies in a single plastic tarp before hauling them out for collection. And Lilac Springs's skin was still shiny red and raw-looking, like the skin on top of a blister. Her hair, which was buzzed short like all the other replicas', was patchy. Some of her scalp showed through.

'It's not so bad,' Lilac Springs said, even though Lyra still hadn't responded. 'Palmolive came.'

Palmolive was also a Brown. She had started throwing up a few weeks ago and was found wandering the halls in the middle of the night. She had been transferred to the Box when she could hardly choke down a few sips of water without bringing it up again.

'Do you think I'll be dead soon?' Lilac Springs asked.

Fortunately, the nurses came in before Lyra had to answer. Lazy Ass and Go Figure were administering. They almost always did. But earlier, Lyra had been afraid that it might be somebody else.

Today there were three tests. Whenever Lyra's heart beat faster, she imagined its four valves opening and closing like shutters, the flow of blood in one direction, an endless loop like all the interlocking wings of Haven. She had learned about hearts like she'd learned about the rest of the human body: because there was nothing else *to* learn, no truth at Haven except for the physical, nothing besides pain and response, symptom and treatment, breathe in and breathe out and skin stretched over muscle over bone.

First, Nurse Go Figure called out a series of five letters and asked that the replicas memorize them. Then they had to rearrange colored slips of paper until they formed a progression, from green to yellow. Then they had to fit small wooden pieces in similarly shaped holes, a ridiculously easy test, although Lilac Springs seemed to be struggling with it – trying to fit the diamond shape into the triangular hole, and periodically dropping pieces so they landed, clatteringly, to the floor.

For the last test, Go Figure distributed papers and pens – Lyra held the pen up to her tongue surreptitiously, enjoying the taste of the ink; she wanted another pen badly for her collection – and asked that the replicas write down the five letters they'd memorized, in order. Most of the replicas had learned their numbers to one hundred

and the alphabet *A* through *Z*, both so they could identify their individual beds and for use in testing, and Lyra
took great pleasure in drawing the curves and angles of
each number in turn, imagining that numbers, too, were
like a language. When she looked up, she saw that Lilac
Springs's paper was still completely blank. Lilac Springs
was holding her pen clumsily, staring at it as though she'd
never seen one. She hadn't even remembered a single letter, although Lyra knew she knew her numbers and was
very proud of it.

Then Lazy Ass called time, and Nurse Go Figure collected the papers, and they sat in silence as the results
were collected, tabulated, and marked in their files. Lyra's
palms began to sweat. Now.

'I forgot the letters,' Lilac Springs said. 'I couldn't
remember the letters.'

'All right, that's it.' Lazy Ass hauled herself out of her
chair, wincing, as she always did after testing. The replicas stood, too. Only Lyra remained sitting, her heart
clenching and unclenching in her chest.

As always, as soon as Lazy Ass was on her feet, she started
complaining: 'Goddamn shoes. Goddamn weather. And
now my lazy ass gotta go all the way to Admin. Take me
twenty minutes just to get there and back. And those men
coming today.' Lazy Ass normally worked the security
desk and subbed in to help with testing when she had

to. She was at least one hundred pounds overweight, and her ankles swelled in the heat until they were thick and round as the trunks of the palms that lined the garden courtyard.

'Go figure,' said Go Figure, like she always did. She had burnished brown skin that always looked as if it had been recently oiled.

Now. Most of the other replicas had left. Only Lilac Springs remained, still seated, staring at the table.

'I'll do it,' Lyra said. She felt breathless even though she hadn't moved, and she wondered whether Lazy Ass would notice. But no. Of course she wouldn't. Many of the nurses couldn't even tell the replicas apart. When she was a kid, Lyra remembered staring at the nurses, willing them to stare back at her, to *see* her, to take her hand or pick her up or tell her she was pretty. She had once been moved to solitary for two days after she stole Nurse Em's security badge, thinking that the nurse wouldn't be able to leave at the end of the day, that she would *have* to stay. But Nurse Em had found a way to leave, of course, and soon afterward she had left Haven forever.

Lyra had gotten used to it: to all the leaving, to being left. Now she was glad to be invisible. They were invisible to her, too, in a way. That was why she'd given them nicknames.

Nurse Go Figure and Lazy Ass turned, staring. Lyra's

face was hot. *Rosacea.* She knew it all from a lifetime of listening to the doctors.

'What'd it say?' Lazy Ass said, very slowly. She wasn't talking to Lyra, but Lyra answered anyway.

'It can do it,' Lyra said, forcing herself to stay very still. When she was little, she'd been confused about the difference between *I* and *it* and could never keep them straight. Sometimes when she was nervous, she still slipped up. She tried again. 'I can bring the files to Admin for you.'

Go Figure snorted. 'Jesus, Mary, and Joseph,' she said.

But Lazy Ass kept staring, as though seeing Lyra for the first time. 'You know how to get to Admin?'

Lyra nodded. She had always lived at Haven. She would always live at Haven. There were many rooms locked, forbidden, accessible only by key cards and codes – many places she couldn't enter, many closed doors behind which people moved, helmeted, suited up in white. But she knew all the lengths of the hallways and the time it took in seconds to get from the toilet to the Stew Pot and back; knew the desks and break rooms, stairways and back ways, like she knew the knobs of her own hips or the feel of the bed, number 24, that had always been hers. Like she knew Omiron and latex, Invacare Snake Tubing and Red Caps and the Glass Eyes.

Her friends, her enemies, her *world.*

'What's Admin, Lyra?' Lilac Springs asked. She was

going to ruin everything – and she knew where Admin was. Everybody did. Even Lilac Springs wasn't that dumb.

'I'll be quick,' Lyra said, ignoring Lilac Springs.

'Dr. Sappo won't like it,' Go Figure said. Dr. Sappo was what the staff called God, but only when he couldn't hear them. Otherwise they called him Dr. Saperstein or Director Saperstein. 'They ain't supposed to get their hands on nothing important.'

Lazy Ass snorted. 'I don't care if he do or don't like it,' she said. 'He ain't got blisters the size of Mount St. Helens on both feet. Besides, he won't know one way or the other.'

'What if it messes up?' Go Figure said. 'Then you'll be in trouble.'

'I won't,' Lyra protested, and then cleared her throat when her voice came out as a croak. 'Mess it up, I mean. I know what to do. I go down to Sub-One in A-Wing.'

Lilac Springs began to whine. 'I want to go to Admin.'

'Uh-uh,' Nurse Go Figure said, turning to Lilac Springs. 'This one's coming with me.' And then, in a low voice, but not so low both Lilac Springs and Lyra couldn't hear: 'The Browns are going like flies. It's funny how it hits them all differently.'

'That's because they ain't got it right yet.' Lazy Ass shook her head. 'All's I know is they better be for real about how it doesn't catch.' She was still watching Lyra through half-narrowed eyes, evaluating, drumming the stack of test results as if an answer might come through her fingertips.

'I've told you, it isn't contagious. Not like that, anyway. I've been here since the start. Do I look dead to you?'

Lilac Springs began to cry – loudly, a high, blubbering wail, like the cry of one of the infant replicas in the observation units. Go Figure had to practically drag her to her feet and out into the hall. Only when Lyra could no longer hear Lilac Springs's voice did she realize she'd been holding her breath.

Lazy Ass slid the papers a half inch toward her. Lyra stood up so quickly the chair jumped across the tile floor.

'Straight through and no stopping,' Lazy Ass said. 'And if anyone asks you where you're going, keep walking and mind your own business. Should be Werner down at the desk. Tell him I sent you.'

Lyra could feel the muscles around her lips twitching. But Lazy Ass would be suspicious if she looked too happy. She took the papers – even the *sound* of paper was delicious – and held them carefully to her chest.

'Go on,' Lazy Ass said.

Lyra didn't want to wait, fearing Lazy Ass would change her mind. Even after she'd turned into the hall, she kept waiting for the nurse to shout, to call her back, to decide it was a bad idea. The linoleum was cold on her bare feet.

Haven consisted of six wings, A–G. There was no E-Wing, for reasons no one understood, although rumor among the staff was that the first God, Richard Haven, had an ex-wife named Ellen. Except for the Box, officially called G-Wing, all the buildings were interconnected, arranged in a pentagon formation around a four-acre courtyard fitted with gardens and statues, benches, and even a paddleball court for staff use. Electronic double doors divided the wings at each juncture, like a series of mechanized elbows. Only the Box was larger – four stories at least, and as many as three more, supposedly, underground, although given that they were at sea level, that seemed unlikely. It was detached, situated a solid hundred yards away from Haven proper and built of gray cement.

The fastest way to A-Wing from the testing rooms was through F-Wing. She'd already decided that if anyone asked, she'd say she was on her way to the Stew Pot for lunch.

But no one asked. She passed several nurses sitting in the dayroom, laughing about two women on TV – replicas, Lyra thought, with a quick spark of excitement, until she recognized from small differences between them that they were just twins. Then came the dorms: smaller rooms for the lower staff, where nurses and researchers might sleep as many as four to a room, bunk-style; then the doctors' quarters, which were more spacious. Finally, the Stew Pot. The smell of cooked meat immediately made her stomach turn.

She hurried on, keeping her head down. When she buzzed into A-Wing, the guard on duty barely glanced up. She passed through the marble lobby with its stone bust of Richard Haven, the first God, which someone had draped in a red-and-blue cape and outfitted with a funny-looking hat: it was some game, Lyra understood, something to do with a place called U Penn, where both the first and second Gods had come from. A plastic Christmas tree, originally purchased for Haven's annual party, had for three years stood just inside the main entryway, though during the off-season it was unplugged. Photographs of strangers smiled down from the walls, and in one of them Richard Haven and Dr. Saperstein were much younger and dressed in red and blue. They even had their faces painted.

Today, however, she didn't stop to look. She pushed through the doors that led into the stairwell. It smelled faintly of cigarettes.

The closer she got to Admin, the greater the pressure on her chest, as if there were Invacare Snake Tubing threaded down her throat, pumping liquid into her lungs. Sub-One was always quieter than the ground floor of Haven. Most of the doors down here were fitted with control pads and marked with big red circles divided in two on the diagonal, signs that they were restricted-access only. Plus, the walls seemed to vacuum up noise, absorbing the sound of Lyra's footsteps as soon as she moved.

Administration was restricted-access, too. Lazy Ass had said Werner would be behind the desk, and Lyra's whole plan depended on it. Twin windows in the door looked into a space filled with individual office cubicles: flyers pinned to corkboard, keyboards buried under piles of manila files, phones and computers cabled to overloaded power strips. All of Haven's paperwork came here, from mail to medical reports, before being routed and redirected to its ultimate destination.

Lyra ducked into an alcove twenty feet beyond the entrance to Admin. If she peeked into the hall, she had a clear view of the doors. She prayed she had arrived on time and hadn't missed her chance. Several times, she inched into the hall to check. But the doors were firmly shut.

Finally, when Lyra had nearly given up hope, she heard a faint click as the locks released. The doors squeaked open. A second later, footsteps headed for the stairs. As soon as she heard the door to the stairwell open, Lyra slipped into the hall.

Lyra had been occasionally sneaking down to Admin ever since Dr. O'Donnell had vanished abruptly. She knew that every day, when most of the other administrative staff was still eating in the Stew Pot, Werner snuck away from his desk, propped the doors of Admin open, and smoked a cigarette – sometimes two – in the stairwell.

Today he had wedged an empty accordion file into the double doors to keep them from closing. Lyra slipped inside, making sure the accordion file stayed in place, and closed the door gently behind her.

For a few seconds, she stood very still, allowing the silence to enfold her. Administration was actually several interconnected rooms. This, the first of them, brightly modern, was fitted with long ceiling lights similar to the ones used in the labs upstairs. Lyra moved deeper, into the forest of file cabinets and old plastic storage bins, into mountains of paperwork no one had touched for years. A few rooms were dark, or only partly illuminated. And she could hear, in the quiet, the whisper of millions of words, words trapped behind every drawer, words beating their fingernails against the inside of the file cabinets.

All the words she could ever want: words to stuff herself on until she was full, until her eyes burst.

She moved to the farthest corner of the dimmest room and picked a file cabinet at random. She didn't care about the actual reports, about what they might say or mean.

All she cared about was the opportunity to practice. Dr. O'Donnell had explained to her once what a *real* library was, and the function it served in the outside world, and Lyra knew Admin was the closest she would ever get.

She selected a file from the very back – one she was sure hadn't been touched in a long time, slender enough to conceal easily. She closed the cabinet and went carefully back the way she had come, through rooms that grew ever lighter and less dusty.

Then she was in the hall. She slipped into the alcove and waited. Sure enough, less than a minute later, the door to the stairwell squeaked open and clanged shut, and footsteps came down the hall. Werner was back.

She had yet to fulfill her official errand. That meant concealing the hard-won file somewhere, if only for a little while. There weren't many options. She chose a metal bin mounted on the wall marked with a sign she recognized as meaning *hazardous*. Normally the nurses and doctors used them for discarding used gloves, caps, and even syringes, but this one was empty.

Werner didn't even let her in. He came to the door, frowning, when she tapped a finger to the glass.

'What is it?' he said. His voice was muffled through the glass, but he spoke very slowly, as if he wasn't sure Lyra could understand. He wasn't used to dealing with replicas. That was obvious.

'Shannon from security sent me,' she said, stopping herself at the last second from saying *Lazy Ass*.

Werner disappeared. When he returned to open the door, she saw that he had suited up in gloves and a face mask. It wasn't unusual for members of the staff to refuse to interact with the replicas unless they were protected, which Lyra thought was stupid. The diseases that killed the replicas, the conditions that made them small and slow and stupid, were directly related to the cloning process and to being raised at Haven.

He looked at the file in her hand as if it was something dead. 'Go on. Give it. And tell *Shannon from security* to do her own work next time.' He snatched the file from her and quickly withdrew, scowling at her from behind the glass. She barely noticed. Already, in her head, she was curling up inside all those letters – new pages, new words to decipher and trip over and decode.

She retrieved the file from the metal bin after checking to see that she was still alone. This was the only part of the plan she hadn't entirely thought out. She had to get the file up to her bed, but if she carried it openly, someone *might* wonder where it had come from. She could say a nurse had given it to her to deliver – but what if someone checked? She wasn't even sure whether she could lie convincingly. She hadn't spoken to the staff so much in years, and she was already exhausted.

Instead she opted to slip it under the waistband of her standard-issue pants, pouching her shirt out over it. The only way to keep it from slipping was to wrap both arms around her stomach, as if she had a bad stomachache. Even then, she had to take small steps, and she imagined that the sound of crinkling paper accompanied her. But she had no choice. Hopefully, she would make it back to D-Wing without having to speak to anyone.

But no sooner had she passed through the doors into the stairwell than she heard the sound of echoing voices. Before she could retreat, God came down the stairs with one of the Suits. Lyra ducked her head and stepped aside, squeezing her arms close around the file, praying they would move past her without stopping.

They stopped.

'Hey.' It was the stranger who spoke. 'Hey. You.' His eyes were practically black. He turned to God. 'Which one is this?'

'Not sure. Some of the nurses can tell them apart on sight.' God looked at Lyra. 'Which one are you?' he asked.

Maybe it was the stolen file pressed to her stomach, but Lyra had the momentary impulse to introduce herself by name. Instead she said, 'Number twenty-four.'

'And you just let them wander around like this?' The man was still staring at Lyra, but obviously addressing himself to God. 'Even after what happened?' Lyra knew he must be talking about the Code Black.

'We're following protocols,' God said. God's voice reminded Lyra of the bite of the syringes. 'When Haven started, it was important to the private sector that they be treated humanely.'

'There is no private sector. We're the ones holding the purse strings now,' the man said. 'What about contagion?'

Lyra was only half listening. Sweat was gathering in the space between the folder and her stomach. She imagined it seeping through the folder, dampening the pages. The folder had shifted fractionally and she was worried a page might escape, but she didn't dare adjust her grip.

'There's no risk except through direct ingestion – as you would know, if you actually read the reports. All right, twenty-four,' God said. 'You can go.'

Lyra was so relieved she could have shouted. Instead she lowered her head and, keeping her arms wrapped tightly around her waist, started to move past them.

'Wait.'

The Suit called out to her. Lyra stiffened and turned around to face him on the stairs. They were now nearly eye to eye. She felt the same way she did during examinations, shivering in her paper gown, staring up at the high unblinking lights set in the ceiling: cold and exposed.

'What's the matter with its stomach?' he asked.

Lyra tightened her hands around her waist. *Please,* she thought. *Please.* She couldn't complete the thought. If she were forced to move her arms, the file would drop. She imagined papers spilling from her pants legs, tumbling down the stairs.

God indicated the plastic wristband Lyra always wore. 'Green,' he said. 'One of the first variants. Slower-acting than your typical vCJD. Most of the Greens are still alive, although we've seen a few signs of neurodegenerative activity recently.'

'So what's that mean in English?'

Unlike the man in the suit, God never made eye contact. He looked at her shoulders, her arms, her kneecaps, her forehead: everywhere but her eyes.

'Side effects,' he said, with a thin smile. Then Lyra was free to go.

Lyra wasn't the only replica that collected things. Rose kept used toothbrushes under her pillow. Palmolive scanned the hallways for dropped coins and stored them in a box that had once contained antibacterial swabs. Cassiopeia had lined up dozens of seashells on the windowsill next to her bed, and additionally had convinced Nurse Dolly to sneak her some Scotch tape so she could hang several drawings she'd created on napkins stolen from the mess hall. She drew Dumpsters and red-barred circles and stethoscopes and the bust of the first God in his red-and-blue cape and scalpels gleaming in folds of clean cloth. She was very good. Calliope had once taken a cell phone from one of the nurses, and all her genotypes had been punished for it.

But Lyra was careful with her things. She was *private* about them. The file folder she hid carefully under her thin mattress, next to her other prized possessions: several pens, including her favorite, a green one with a retractable tip that said *Fine & Ives* in block white lettering; an empty tin that read *Altoids*; a half-dozen coins she'd found behind the soda machine; her worn and battered copy of *The Little Prince*, which she'd handled so often that many of the pages had come loose from their binding.

'There's a message in this book,' Dr. O'Donnell had told Lyra, before leaving Haven. 'In the love of the Little Prince for his rose, there's wisdom we could all learn from.' And Lyra had nodded, trying to pretend she understood, even though she didn't understand. Not about love. Not about hope. Dr. O'Donnell was going away, and once again, Lyra was left behind.

FIVE

'YOU'VE BEEN LYING TO ME, twenty-four.'

Lyra was on her knees, blinking back tears, swallowing the taste of vomit, when the closet door opened. She couldn't get to her feet fast enough. She spun around, accidentally knocking over a broom with her elbow.

Nurse Curly was staring not at Lyra but at the bucket behind her, now splattered with vomit. Strangely, she didn't seem angry. 'I knew it,' she said, shaking her head.

It was early afternoon, and Curly must have just arrived from the launch for the shift change. She wasn't yet wearing her scrubs, but a blue tank top with beading at the shoulders, jeans, and leather sandals. Usually, Lyra was mesmerized by evidence of life outside Haven – the occasional magazine, water-warped, abandoned on the sink in the nurses' toilets; used-up lip balm in the trash; or a broken flip-flop sitting on a bench in the courtyard – split-second fissures through which a whole other world was revealed.

Today, however, she didn't care.

She'd been so sure that here, in a rarely used janitorial closet in D-Wing Sub-One, she'd be safe. She'd woken up sweating, with her heart going hard and her stomach like something heavy and raw that needed to come out. But the waking bell sounded only a minute later, and she knew that the bathrooms would soon be full of replicas showering, brushing their teeth, whispering beneath the thunderous sound of the water about the Suits and what they could possibly want and whether number 72 had been torn apart by alligators by now – lungs, kidneys, spleen scattered across the marshes.

But the staff bathrooms were just as risky. They were off-limits, first of all, and often crowded – the nurses were always hiding out in stalls trying to make calls or send text messages.

'I'm not sick,' Lyra said quickly, reaching out to grab hold of a shelf. She was still dizzy.

'Come on, now.' As usual Nurse Curly acted as if she hadn't heard. Maybe she hadn't. Lyra had the strangest sense of being invisible, as if she existed behind a curtain and the nurses and doctors could only vaguely see her. 'We'll go to Dr. Levy.'

'No. Please.' Dr. Levy worked in the Box. She hated him, and that big, thunderous machine, Mr. I. She hated the grinning lights like blank indifferent faces. She hated Catheter Fingers and Invacare Snake Tubing, Dribble Bags and Sad Sacks, syringe after syringe after syringe. She hated the weird dreams that visited her there, of lions marching around a cylindrical cup, of old voices she was sure she'd never heard but that felt real to her. Even a spinal tap with the Vampire – the long needle inserted into the base of her spinal column between two vertebrae so that her fluids could be extracted for testing – was almost preferable. 'I feel fine.'

'Don't be silly,' Curly said. 'It's for your own good. Come on out of there.'

Lyra edged into the hall, keeping her hands on the walls, which were studded with nails from which brooms and mops and dustpans were hanging. She couldn't remember what day it was. The knowledge seemed to have dropped through a hole in her awareness. She couldn't remember what day yesterday had been, either, or what had happened.

'Follow me.' The nurse put her hand on Lyra's arm, and Lyra was overwhelmed. It was rare that the nurses touched them unless they had to, in order to take their measurements. Lyra's knowledge of the nurse's name had evaporated, too, though she was sure she had known it just a second earlier. What was happening to her? It was as if vomiting had shaken up all the information in her brain, muddled it.

Lyra's eyes were burning and her throat felt raw. When she reached up to wipe her mouth, she was embarrassed to realize she was crying.

'It's normal,' the nurse said. Lyra wasn't sure what she meant.

It was quicker from here to go through C-Wing, where the male replicas were kept. Nurse Cheryl – the name came back to Lyra suddenly, loosed from the murky place it had been stuck – Nurse Cheryl, nicknamed Curly for her hair, which corkscrewed around her face, buzzed them in. Lyra hung back. In all her years at Haven, she'd only been through C-Wing a few times. She hadn't forgotten Pepper, and what had happened. She remembered how Pepper had cried when she'd first been told what was happening to her, that she would be a *birther*, like all those dark-skinned women who came and left on boats and were never seen outside the barracks. Pepper had left fingernail scratches across the skin of her belly and begged for the doctors to get it out.

But two months later, by the time the doctors determined she couldn't keep it, she was already talking names: Ocean, Sunday, Valium. After Pepper, all the knives in the mess hall were replaced with plastic versions, and the male and female replicas were kept even more strictly apart.

'It's okay.' Curly gave her a nudge. 'Go on. You're with me.'

It was hotter in C-Wing. Or maybe Lyra was just hot. In the first room they passed she saw a male replica, lying on an examination table with probes attached to his bare chest. She looked away quickly. It smelled different in C-Wing – the same mixture of antiseptic and bleach and human sweat, but deeper somehow.

They took the stairs up to ground level and moved past a series of dorms, lined with cots just like on the girls' side and mercifully empty. The males who weren't sick or in testing were likely getting fed in Stew Pot. Despite the standard-issue white sheets and gray blankets, and the plastic under-bed bins, the rooms managed to give an impression of messiness.

They passed into B-Wing, and Curly showed her credentials to two guards on duty. B-Wing was for research and had restricted access. Passed laboratories, dazzling white, illuminated by rows and rows of fluorescent light, where more researchers were working, moving slowly in their gloves and lab coats, hair concealed beneath translucent gray caps, eyes magnified, insect-like, by their goggles. Banks of computers, screens filled with swirling colors, hard metal equipment, words Lyra had heard her whole life without ever knowing what they meant – spectrometry, biometrics, liquid chromatography – beautiful words, words to trip over and fall into.

One time, she had worked up the courage to ask Dr. O'Donnell what they did all day in the research rooms. It didn't seem possible that all those men and women were there just to perfect the replication process, to keep the birthers from miscarrying so often after the embryo transfer, to keep the replicas from dying so young.

Dr. O'Donnell had hesitated. 'They're studying what makes you sick,' she said at last, speaking slowly, as if she had to carefully handle the words or they would cut her. 'They're studying how it works, and how long it takes, and why.'

'And how to fix it?' Lyra had asked.

Dr. O'Donnell had barely hesitated. 'Of course.'

The Box was made of concrete slab, sat several hundred yards away from the main complex, and was enclosed by its own fence. Unlike the rest of Haven, the G-Wing had no windows, and extra security required Nurse Curly to identify herself twice and show her badge to various armed guards who patrolled the perimeter.

Curly left Lyra in the entrance foyer, in front of the elevator that gave access to Sub-One and, supposedly, the concealed subterranean levels. Lyra tried not to look at the doors that led to the ER, where so many replicas died or *failed to thrive* in the first place. Even the nurses called

REPLICA

46

REPLICA

the G-Wing the Funeral Home or the Graveyard. Lyra wondered whether Lilac Springs was there even now, and how long she had left.

Soon enough, the elevator doors opened and a technician wearing a heavy white lab coat, her hair concealed beneath a cap, arrived to escort Lyra down to see Mr. I. It was, as far as Lyra could tell, the same tech she'd seen the half-dozen or so times she'd been here in the past month. Then again, she had trouble telling them apart, since their faces were so often concealed behind goggles and a mask, and since they never spoke directly to her.

In Sub-One, they walked down a long, windowless hallway filled with doors marked *Restricted*. But when a researcher slipped out into the hall, Lyra had a brief view of a sanitation room and, beyond it, a long, galley-shaped laboratory in which dozens of researchers were bent over gleaming equipment, dressed in head-to-toe protective clothing and massive headgear that made them look like the pictures of astronauts Lyra had occasionally seen on the nurses' TV.

Mr. I sat by itself in a cool bright room humming with recirculated air. To Lyra, Mr. I looked like an open mouth, and the table on which she was supposed to lie down a long pale tongue. The hair stood up on her arms and legs.

'Remember to stay very still,' the tech said, her voice

muffled by a paper mask. 'Otherwise we'll just have to start over. And nobody wants that, do we?'

Afterward she was transferred to a smaller room and told to lie down. Sometimes lying this way, with doctors buzzing above her, she lost track of whether she was a human at all or some other thing, a slab of meat or a glass overturned on a countertop. A thing.

'I don't believe Texas is any further than we are. It's bullshit. They're bluffing. Two years ago, they were still infecting bovine tissue –'

'It doesn't matter if they're bluffing if our funding gets cut. Everyone *thinks* they're closer. Fine and Ives loses the contract. Then we're shit outta luck.'

High bright lights, cool sensors moving over her body, gloved hands pinching and squeezing. 'Sappo thinks the latest variant will do it. I'm talking full progression within a *week*. Can you imagine the impact?'

'He better be right. What the hell will we do with all of them if we get shut down? Ever think of that?'

Lyra closed her eyes, suddenly exhausted.

'Open your eyes, please. Follow my finger, left to right. Good.'

'Reflexes still look okay.' One of the doctors, the woman, parted her paper gown and squeezed her nipple, hard. Lyra cried out. 'And pain response. Do me a favor – check this one's file, will you? What variant is this?'

'This is similar to the vCJD, just slower-acting. That's why the pulvinar sign is detectable on the MRI. Very rare in nature, nearly always inherited.'

They worked in silence for a bit. Lyra thought about *The Little Prince*, and Dr. O'Donnell, and distant stars where beautiful things lived and died in freedom. She couldn't stop crying.

'How do they choose which ones end up in control, and which ones get the different variants?' the male doctor asked after a while.

'Oh, it's all automated,' the woman said. Now she held Lyra's eyes open with two fingers, ensuring she couldn't blink. 'Okay, come see this. See the way her left eye is spasming? Myoclonus. That's another indicator.'

'Mm–hmm. So it's random?'

'Totally random. The computer does it by algorithm. That way, you know, no one feels bad. Pass me the stethoscope, will you? I bet its heart rate is through the roof.'

That night was very still, and the sound of chanting voices and drumbeats – louder, always, on the days the Suits had visited the island – carried easily over the water. Lyra lay awake for a long time, fighting the constant pull of nausea, listening to the distant rhythm, which didn't sound so distant after all. At times, she imagined it was coming closer, that suddenly Haven would be overrun with strangers. She imagined all of them made of darkness and shadow instead of blood and muscle and bones. She wondered, for the first time, whether number 72 was maybe not dead after all. She remembered hearing once that the marshes were submerged islands, miles of land that had over time been swallowed up by the water.

She wondered whether 72 had been swallowed up too, or whether he was out there somewhere, listening to the voices.

She took comfort in the presence of the new addition to her collection, buried directly beneath her lower back. She imagined that the file pushed up heat, like a heart, like the warmth of Dr. O'Donnell's touch. *98.6 degrees Fahrenheit.* She imagined the smell of lemon and antiseptic, as if Dr. O'Donnell were still there, floating between the beds.

'Don't worry,' Dr. O'Donnell had once said to her on a night like this one, when the voices were louder than usual. 'They can't get to you,' she'd said more quietly. 'They can't get in.'

But about this, Dr. O'Donnell was wrong.

SIX

LYRA DID NOT SLEEP WELL. She woke up with a tight, airless feeling in her chest, like the time years ago when Nurse Don't-Even-Think-About-It had held Lyra's head in the sink to punish her for stealing some chocolate from the nurses' break room.

Side effects. They would pass. Medicines sometimes made you sick before they made you better. In the dim morning light, with the sound of so many replicas inhaling and exhaling beside her, she closed her eyes. She had a brief memory of a birther rocking her years ago, singing to her, the tickle of hair on her forehead. She opened her eyes again. The birthers didn't sing. They howled and screamed. Or they wept. They spoke in other languages. But they didn't sing.

She was nauseous again.

This time she wouldn't risk throwing up inside. She

would have to find someplace more remote – along the beach, maybe behind the tin drums of hazardous waste Haven lined up for collection, somewhere the guards couldn't see her.

She chose to pass through the courtyard, which was mostly empty. Many of the night nurses would be preparing to take the launch back to Cedar Key. She passed the statue of the first God, Richard Haven. It dominated the center of the yard, where all four walking paths intersected. Here she rested, leaning against the cool marble base, next to a plaque commemorating his work and achievements. He'd had a kind face, Lyra thought. At least, the artist had given him one.

She didn't remember the flesh-and-blood man. He'd died before she was made. The sculptor had depicted him kneeling, with one arm raised. Lyra guessed he was supposed to be calling out to invisible crowds to *come*, to *look here*, but to her it had always looked as if he was stretching one arm toward the clouds, toward the other God, the ones the nurses believed in. Their God, too, hated the replicas.

She squatted next to twin drums marked with a biohazard symbol and threw up into the high grasses that grew between them. She felt slightly better when she stood up, but still weak. She stopped a half-dozen times during the walk back to the main building, earning a disapproving glance from one of the patrolling guards. Normally, she was grateful for the sheer size of Haven, for the tracts of open space and the walkways shaded by hickory trees and high palmettos, for the bright bursts of heliotrope in the flower beds, and the wild taro pushing between the cement paving stones, although she had names for none of them and knew the growth only in general terms: flowers, trees, plants. But today she was exhausted and wished simply to get back to bed 24.

She heard shouting as she entered D-Wing. As Lyra got closer to the dorm, she recognized one of the voices: Dr. Saperstein. She nearly stopped and turned around. God had never come to the bunks, ever.

But then she heard Cassiopeia shout, 'Don't touch them. It's not *fair*,' and she kept going.

Up ahead, a nurse hurried out into the hall, skidding a little on the tile, and shot Lyra a strange look before scurrying in the opposite direction, leaving the dorm room door swinging open. Lyra barely caught it before it closed.

Then she stopped, her breath catching. Cassiopeia was on her hands and knees in front of Dr. Saperstein, trying to sweep up her collection of shells, which had been knocked off the windowsill and shattered. All of the individual drawings pasted to the wall behind her bed had been torn down, as if a hard wind had come ripping through the bunk, though it hadn't disturbed anything else. Then Lyra saw he was holding them, crumpled together in his fist.

'Unbelievable.' He was shouting, but not at the girls. Instead he was yelling at the assembled nursing staff, including Nurse Dolly, who'd found Cassiopeia Scotch tape so they could hang the napkins in the first place. 'Do you know how close we are to getting defunded? Do you want to be out of a job? We have a quota, we have protocols –'

'It was my fault,' Nurse Dolly said. 'I didn't see any harm in it.'

God took a step toward her, nearly tripping over Cassiopeia, who was still on the floor, crying softly. Lyra wanted to go to her but found she couldn't move. God's shoes crunched quietly on the carpet of shattered seashells.

'No harm in it?' he repeated, and Nurse Dolly quickly looked away. Now he was speaking softly, but strangely, and Lyra was more frightened of him than ever. 'I've worked my whole career to see this project succeed. We're doing some of the most important medical work of the past two decades, and yet –' He broke off, shaking his head. '*Results.* That's what we need. *Results.* This is a research facility, not a playpen. Is that clear to everyone?'

No one spoke. In the silence, Lyra could hear her heart. *Boom-boom-boom.* Like the rhythm of the chanting that carried all the way to Spruce Island from Barrel Key.

Monsters, monsters. Burn Haven down.

God sighed. He took off his glasses and rubbed his eyes. 'We're doing important work,' he said. 'Good work. Never forget that.' He started to turn away and then stopped. 'It's better this way – for everyone.'

But Lyra knew, from the tone of his voice, that he didn't mean the replicas.

God had to step around Cassiopeia again to move to the door. He barely glanced at her. Instead he kicked at a seashell, sending it skittering across the floor. 'Someone clean up this mess, please,' he announced, to no one in particular. Lyra stepped quickly out of the doorway to avoid him.

For a long moment after he was gone, no one moved. Just Cassiopeia, still sorting through the remains of her collection, now reduced to shards and dust. Finally Nurse Dolly went to her.

'All right,' she said, crouching down and grabbing Cassiopeia's wrist to stop her from reaching for another broken shell. 'That's enough now.'

It happened so quickly: Cassiopeia turned and *shoved* Nurse Dolly. 'Get off me,' she said, and several people cried out, and Lyra took a step forward, saying, '*Don't.*'

Maybe she hadn't meant to push Nurse Dolly hard, or maybe she had. Either way, Nurse Dolly lost her balance and went backward. In an instant, Nurse

Don't-Even-Think-About-It had crossed to Cassiopeia and wrenched her to her feet.

'Wicked thing,' Don't-Even-Think-About-It spat at her, keeping hold of her wrists. 'How dare you touch her – how dare you, when we've fed and clothed and kept you all these years? The judgment of God will come for you, don't you forget it.'

'You don't own me.' Cassiopeia's eyes were very bright and she was shaking. Lyra stared at her, filled with a sudden sense of dread. She didn't understand what Cassiopeia meant – she didn't understand where she'd found these words, this anger, and for a second she felt as if the room was splitting apart, revealing a dark gulf, a hidden fault line. 'You can't tell me what to do. I don't belong to you. I'm real. I am.'

'You're not anything,' Don't-Even-Think-About-It said. Her face was mottled with anger, like the veined slabs of beef shelved in the kitchen freezers. 'You belong to the institute, and to Dr. Saperstein. You can stay here, or you can leave and be killed.'

'I'll be killed anyway.' Cassiopeia looked almost happy, as if she'd successfully passed her Cog Testing, and Lyra didn't know why, knew that couldn't be right. Goose-down, one of Cassiopeia's other genotypes, stood hugging herself, as if she were the one getting yelled at. They were identical except for the vacancy of Goosedown's expression. She'd had a habit, when she was little, of smacking her own head against the ground when she was frustrated, and she still had to wear diapers to sleep. 'Isn't that right? We'll all die here eventually. What's the difference?'

'Let it go, Maxine.' Nurse Dolly was climbing to her feet, wincing, holding on to her lower back. Lyra was unaccountably angry at Cassiopeia. Nurse Dolly was one of the nicest ones. 'It doesn't understand.'

Nurse Don't-Even-Think-About-It stood for a moment, still gripping Cassiopeia's wrists. Then, abruptly, she released her and turned away. 'Unnatural,' she muttered. 'Devil's work, all of it.'

'Enough.' Nurse Curly spoke up this time, addressing everyone. 'You two' – she pointed at Goosedown and Bounty, still watching, frozen – 'help number six clean up.'

But Cassiopeia bolted for the door instead, pushing past Nurse Don't-Even-Think-About-It and shaking Lyra off when Lyra went to touch her arm.

'Grab it!' Don't-Even-Think-About-It shouted, but Nurse Dolly shook her head.

'She'll be back.' She sighed. She looked exhausted. There were dark circles under her eyes, and Lyra found herself wondering briefly about the nurse's other life, the one off the island. What would it be like to have a secret world, a private place away from Haven, away from the replicas and the nurses and the Glass Eyes? She couldn't fathom it.

Nurse Dolly met Lyra's eyes, and Lyra looked quickly away.

'There's nowhere for her to run, anyway,' Nurse Dolly added, but gently, as if in apology.

Cassiopeia wasn't at lunch. The replicas didn't speak about her. They didn't speak at all. It was difficult to feel comfortable surrounded by half the nursing staff and several guards, all of them posted around the perimeter of the room, silent, expressionless, watching the girls eat, many of them wearing masks or full hazmat suits that made them resemble inflated balloons.

Lyra had no appetite. She was still nauseous, and the smell of the Stew Pot made her stomach clench, as if it wanted to bring something up. But she didn't risk skipping lunch. She didn't want to go into the Funeral Home. So she lined up with the other replicas and filled her plate with mashed potatoes and chicken floating in a vivid red sauce the electric color of inner organs and pushed her food around, cut it into small pieces, hid some in her napkin.

Lyra needed to find a new hiding place. The dorm was no longer safe. She was responsible for changing her own linens – but what if one day she forgot, and the book and the file, her pen and her Altoids tin, were discovered? They'd be taken away and destroyed, and Lyra would never get over it. The book especially – that was her last piece of Dr. O'Donnell, and the only thing that Lyra had ever been given, except for standard-issue clothing and a scratchy blanket for cool nights.

Lyra headed straight to the bunks after lunch. The dorm was mostly empty: after lunch, the female replicas had a half an hour of free time before afternoon physicals. Only a half-dozen replicas had preceded her back, and there was a single nurse on patrol, Nurse Stink, an older woman who chewed special candies made of ginger and garlic for indigestion, and who always smelled like them as a result.

Lyra went straight to bed 24 and, keeping her back angled to the nurse, began stripping the sheets from the bed. At a certain point, she slid a hand between the mattress and the frame and drew out the book, and then the file, at the same time stuffing them down into a pillow-case so they were invisible. Then she headed for the door, pressing the linens tight to her chest, as if they might help muffle the sound of her heart.

'Where are you going?' the nurse asked. She was sitting in a folding chair by the door, fumbling to unwrap one of her candies.

'The laundry,' Lyra answered, surprised that her voice sounded so steady.

'Laundry day was yesterday,' Nurse Stink said.

'I know,' Lyra said, and lowered her voice. 'But it's my monthly bleeding.'

The nurse waved a hand as if to say, *Go on.*

Lyra turned left to get to the end of D-Wing. But instead of going downstairs to the laundry, she ducked out of the first exit, a fire door that led to the south-eastern side of the institute, where the land sloped very gently toward the fence and the vast marshland beyond it. Birds were wheeling against a pale-blue sky, and the stink of wild taro and dead fish was strong. From here, the marshes were so covered in water lettuce they looked almost like solid ground. But Lyra knew better. She'd been told again and again about the tidal marshes, about fishermen and curiosity seekers and adventurers from Barrel Key who'd lost their way among the tumorous growth and had been found drowned.

Lyra hid the bundle of sheets behind a trimmed hedge. She tucked the pillowcase with her belongings in it under her shirt and kept going, circling the main building. She spotted Cassiopeia, sitting motionless by the fence, staring out over the marshes, hugging her knees to her chest. Lyra thought of going to her but wasn't sure what she would say. And Cassiopeia had caused trouble. She'd pushed Nurse Dolly. She'd be put in solitary or restrained to her bed, kept like that for a day or two. Besides, Lyra was still weak, and even the idea of trying to comfort Cassiopeia exhausted her.

She'd need to find a place not too remote; a place she could sneak off to easily without arousing suspicion, but a place unused for other purposes, where no one else would think to look.

She kept going, toward a portion of the island she'd rarely explored, praying nobody would stop her. She wasn't sure whether she was breaking any rules, and if anyone asked what she was doing or where she was going, she'd have no answer.

The northern half of the island remained undeveloped and largely untouched, since it had, decades earlier, belonged to a timber company. Now it was a repository of old equipment, sealed chemical drums, and trailers mounted on cinder blocks and padlocked off, for the most part, with heavy chains. Lyra paused at a rusted gate hung with a large sign warning of biohazardous material. But the gate was unlocked, and she decided to risk it. Half of Haven contained biohazardous material anyway.

Here there were no neatly trimmed hedges or stone walkways. This area was cooler, shaded by coast oak and mature pines with old, sweeping branches, although to Lyra it all looked the same. As she walked, she thought about animals concealed in dark hiding places, gators crawling up beneath the fence, snakes nesting in the trees. Two years earlier, a wild hog had come bursting out of the undergrowth and run circles around the guards in front of the Box. It was one of the few times Lyra could remember seeing any of the doctors laughing.

Old tractors; rusted, coiled-up chains; plastic garbage bins; Dumpsters; even an old crane, arm raised as if reaching for the sky: Lyra moved down the long alley of broken-down equipment, her feet squelching in mud that became thicker and deeper as she approached the tidal flats. The insects were thicker here, and louder, too. She knew she was still within the limits of Haven – she could see the fence through the trees, and the flashing of the late sun on the vivid green marshes, and knew that the nearest guards were only a few hundred feet away – but she felt almost as if she had entered another world. As if she could keep walking forever, moving deeper and deeper into the trees, and never be found. She didn't know whether the idea excited or scared her.

She spotted an old motorboat, propped up on cinder blocks and covered with a blue plastic tarp slicked with mold and moisture. A perfect hiding place. She felt a rush of sudden relief. She was so tired. For a second, when she stopped walking, she thought she heard footsteps behind her. But when she turned around, she didn't see anyone.

She peeled back a portion of the tarp and froze, confused. The bottom of the boat was spotted with rust but relatively dry – and someone, she saw, was already using it for a hiding place. There was a folded brown blanket, standard Haven issue, as well as two neatly folded changes of pants, two shirts, and two folded pairs of male's underwear. There was, additionally, a flashlight and several cardboard containers of powdered milk, a can opener marked *Property of Haven Kitchens*, and half a dozen cans of soup.

Something stirred in her mind – an association, a *connection* – but before she could bring the idea into focus, someone spoke.

'That's mine,' a voice said behind her. 'Don't touch it.'

She turned and her breath caught in her chest.

Her first thought was that the boy was an outsider and had somehow made his way in. He looked so wild, so *fierce*, she felt he must be a different species. Her second thought was that he was hungry. His cheeks stood out sharply from his face, as if they'd been whittled with a knife. His forearms were marked with little diagonal scars, like a tiny staircase cut into his flesh.

Then she noticed the Haven bracelet – a White – and the idea she'd been reaching for earlier arrived, neat and obvious and undeniable: this was 72. The Code Black. The runaway.

Except he hadn't run away, or at least he hadn't run far. He'd been here, on the north side of the island, the whole time.

'I know you,' she said. 'You're seventy-two.'

He didn't deny it. 'How did you find me?' He took a step toward her, and Lyra could smell him then – a sharp animal smell, not completely unpleasant. 'Which of them sent you?'

'Nobody sent me,' she said. She didn't like being so close to him. She'd never been this close to one of the males, and she couldn't help but think of Pepper, and a diagram she'd seen once of a pregnant woman, who seemed to be digesting her baby. But there was nowhere to go. The side of the boat was digging into her back. 'I wasn't looking for you at all.'

'Then what are you doing here?' he asked.

She hesitated. She was still holding the pillowcase with all her belongings, and she squeezed it to her chest. 'I didn't mean anything by it,' she said.

He shook his head. 'I can't let you go,' he said. He reached out, taking hold of her wrist.

And at that exact moment, the world exploded.

SEVEN

LATER THE RESIDENTS OF BARREL Key would tell
stories about seeing the explosion. Several fishermen,
bringing in their boats, were nearly thrown overboard by
a freak wave that came racing over the sound – caused, it
later turned out, by a portion of A-Wing crashing through
the fence and collapsing into the shallows. Missy Gallagher saw a finger of flame shoot up in the distance and
thought of Revelation and the end of days. Bill Collops
thought of terrorists and ran into the basement, screaming
for his wife to help him with the boxes of ammo.

The first bomb, detonated in the entry hall, directly
next to the bust of Richard Haven, made shrapnel of the
walls and beams and caved in the roof. It killed twenty-
seven staff members, all of them buried under the rubble.
The woman who was carrying the explosives strapped
by means of a cookie sheet to her chest was blown into

so many pieces that even her dental records were useless, and they were able to establish her identity only because she had left a bag explaining her motivations and affiliation with the Angels of the First Savior on the mainland, which would subsequently be discovered by soldiers. Her WordPress account, which referenced at length a website known as the Haven Files, suggested she was acting on directives from Jesus Christ to destroy the unnatural perversions at Haven and purge the sinners playing God. The blog had a brief three-hour surge of notoriety and readership before it was permanently and mysteriously erased.

The second and third bombs created a fireball that roared through the halls, reaching temperatures hot enough to sear metal and leave the plastic dinner trays as molten, shapeless messes. Things would not have been so bad were it not for the close proximity of a large shipment of amyl nitrate, which one of the staff members had signed for and thoughtlessly left still packaged in the entry hall, not entirely sure where it was meant to go.

Later, rumors would circulate: that the bomber believed Haven Institute was actually *manufacturing humans* to use in some kind of devil's army, and that both the creations and their creators should be punished by fire; that she had every single page of the Haven Files, all seventy-six of them, printed out, underlined, annotated, and laminated in her bag next to a copy of the Bible, a small image of

Jesus on the cross, and a half-eaten ham and cheese sand-wich; that she must have been onto something, because of the military crackdown, and the men in hazmat suits who spent weeks sweeping the island, carting off debris, leaving Spruce Island bare and ruined and silent. And why didn't the story make it onto the news, or any of the major newspapers? *Conspiracy,* Bill Collops said, polishing his guns. *What a world,* Missy Gallagher said, shaking her head.

The official story – the one that made it onto the news – stated that chemicals had been mishandled by a new laboratory technician, sparking a huge chemical fire that engulfed the laboratory. But even this story, once estab-lished, was quickly suppressed, and Spruce Island, and what may or may not have happened there, was rapidly forgotten.

Of course Lyra didn't and couldn't know any of this at the time. At the time, she thought the sky had split apart. At the time, she thought the world was ending.

EIGHT

THE FORCE OF THE FIRST blast threw her off her feet. She landed palms-down in the mud, with 72 beside her. Her eyes stung from the sudden vapor of dust, which seemed to rise all at once and everywhere, like a soft exhalation. People were screaming. An alarm kept hitting the same high note of panic, over and over, without end.

It was the sound that paralyzed her: shock waves of sound, a screaming in her ears and the back of her teeth, the sound of atoms splitting in two. It took her a second to realize that 72 was no longer beside her. He was on his feet, running.

But after only a few feet he stopped, and, turning around, saw her still frozen, still belly down in the mud like a salamander. He came back. He had to yell to be heard over the fire and the screaming.

'Move,' he said, but even his words sounded distant, as

if the ringing in her ears had transformed them to vague music. She couldn't move. She was cold and suddenly tired. She wanted to sleep. Even her mouth wouldn't work to say *no*. 'Move now.' She wasn't very good at judging feelings, but she thought he sounded angry.

She was focusing on very small details: the motion of a rock crab scuttling sideways in the churned-up mud, the hiss of wind through the trees that carried the smell of smoke, the male's bare feet an inch from her elbow, his toenails ringed with dirt.

Then 72 had her elbow and she was shocked back into awareness of her body. She felt blood pumping through her heart, valves opening and closing like eyelids inside of her.

'Now,' 72 said again. 'Now, now.' She wondered whether his mind had become stuck on the word, whether like Lilac Springs and Goosedown and so many others his brain had never formed right. She grabbed the pillowcase from the ground where it had fallen. It had gone a dull, gray color, from all the shimmering dust. The Altoids tin landed in the dirt but she had no time to stop and retrieve it. He was still holding on to her elbow, and she wasn't thinking well.

A drumbeat pop-pop-popping sound made her heart lurch, because she knew what it was: every so often the guards, bored, fired at alligators that swam too close to the island. She thought there must be alligators – but the alligators would burn – she wondered whether their hides would protect them. . . .

They went back through the broken machinery, moving not toward the marshes but toward the sound of roaring fire and screams. Ash caught in Lyra's throat and made breathing painful. She didn't think it strange that they were heading back toward the fire – she could see a shimmering haze of smoke in the distance, beyond the trees, smoke that seemed to have taken on the silhouette of a building – because she knew they needed to find a nurse, they needed to line up, they needed to be told what to do. The nurses would tell them. They would make things better. She longed in that moment for Squeezeme and Thermoscan, longed to feel the familiar squeeze of pressure on her arm and suck down the taste of plastic, longed to be back in bed number 24, touching her windowsill, her headboard, her sheets. They moved past the chemical drums and squeezed through the fence through which Lyra had come looking for a hiding place. She was still holding the pillowcase to her chest with one arm and felt a little better, a little more clearheaded.

But as they came into view of the institute, she stopped. For a second she felt one of the bullets must have gone through her, punched a hole directly in her stomach. She could no longer feel her legs. She couldn't understand what she was seeing. It was like someone had smashed up reality and then tried to put it together all wrong. A-Wing was gone and B-Wing was on fire. Flames punched through windows and roared across the tar roof. Guards sprinted across the yard, shouting in voices too distorted to make out.

There were bodies in the grass, human bodies, bodies wearing the sensible flat shoes of the nurses and doctor uniforms stained with blood, arms flung out as if they'd done belly flops to the ground. From a distance, it was impossible to distinguish the people from the replicas except by their clothing.

One body appeared to have been lifted off its feet and carried down toward the beach – Lyra could just see, in the distance, waves breaking against a pair of legs – or maybe someone had been down on the beach when the explosion had come. Lyra thought of Cassiopeia and her seashell collection and, although she had seen replicas die and die and die, felt vomit rise in her throat. *The vomiting center is located in the rear part of the brain.* She had heard that once, from one of the nurses. She didn't remember when.

But now 72 was headed not back to safety, not to the nurses and doctors and gentle Glass Eyes, good Glass Eyes, watchful Glass Eyes, but directly toward one of the guard towers. Now people were pouring from the other wings, nurses and doctors dazed or crying, covered with soot so they looked as if they'd been cast in stone. For the first time, Lyra realized that they, too, were afraid. That none of this was planned. That no one was coming to tell them what to do.

She stumbled on something in her path: a long pale arm, wrist tagged with a green plastic bracelet. The fingers twitched. A female, Lyra thought, because of the shape of the hands. She was buried beneath a heavy sheet of tin siding that had been hurled across the yard by the first explosion. Lyra saw the fingers curl up in a fist: she was alive, whoever she was.

'Wait,' she said, pulling away from 72 and crouching down to try and free the girl. 'Help,' she said, when 72 just stood there, squinting into the distance, looking agitated. He frowned but moved next to her, and together they managed to shift the metal.

Beneath it, Cassiopeia was lying on her back, her face screwed up in pain. Her left leg was twisted at the knee and a gash on her thigh had soaked her pants through with blood. But she was alive. Lyra knelt and touched Cassiopeia's face. Cassiopeia opened her eyes.

'Lyra,' she said, or appeared to say. Her voice was so faint Lyra couldn't hear it.

'Leave it,' 72 said.

'She needs a doctor,' Lyra said, bringing a hand to Cassiopeia's back and helping her sit up. Her hand came away wet and dark with blood. It wasn't just her leg that was injured.

'There are no more doctors. There's no more Haven. It's done,' 72 said. Lyra felt a liquid panic, as if her lungs were slowly filling with water, like in dreams where she was in the ocean and couldn't find her way to the surface.

There was no world without Haven. Haven *was* the world.

And now the world was burning: the flames had spread to C-Wing and waves of heat reached them even from a distance. The guards were still shouting – doctors were crawling on their hands and knees in the dirt – there were replicas in a line, kneeling, hands behind their heads, pinned in place by the guards with their guns – Lyra couldn't understand any of it.

She helped Cassiopeia to her feet. Cassiopeia was sweating and smelled terrible. She had to lean on Lyra heavily and go half shuffling, half hopping across the yard. In the middle of it all Lyra thought how strange it was to be so physically close to someone. She and Cassiopeia had never touched except by accident, when they were washing up at the same sink, and even when they played with the newest crops, to touch and tickle them, it was because they had to. Nurse Em had put an arm around Lyra once, but Lyra couldn't remember why, only that for days afterward she had touched her own shoulder, trying to make it tingle. Even Dr. O'Donnell had never done more than touch Lyra's forehead when she had a fever. This felt like being with Squeezeme, but more, bigger. She wanted to cry.

The guard tower was empty, the post abandoned. The smell of rotten fish and sea kelp was almost overwhelming, as if the smoke had underscored and sharpened it. Lyra at last saw where they were heading: almost directly below the guard tower was an area where the fence had been damaged, yanked out of the ground by winds or by one of the wild hogs that still roamed the island at night.

Seeing that 72 meant to go beneath it, she stopped again, dizzy with the heat and the noise and the harsh animal sounds of screaming. Cassiopeia's breath sounded as if it was being sucked in and out of an air pump, and Lyra could feel Cassiopeia's heart beating hard through her back and ribs, blood racing around to all those fragile veins. But there was a hole somewhere, a puncture. Her shirt was heavy and warm with blood.

Help. She thought the word to no one and to everyone. She knew that people believed in a God who would help them, but God hated the replicas and didn't care whether they lived or died because he hadn't made them. Dr. Saperstein had made them. He was their God. *Help.* She wanted nothing but to return to D-Wing, to lie down in the coolness of the dormitory and pretend nothing had happened.

'If you stay here, you'll die,' 72 said, as if he knew what she was thinking. But he'd released her and no longer seemed to care whether she followed him or not. He went first, sliding on his back feetfirst underneath the gap.

A smell reached her – something sweet and hot she recognized from the Funeral Home as the smell of blood. She looked back at the institute, steadying Cassiopeia on her feet. The dormitories were gone. The peaked roof of A-Wing, normally visible, was gone. In its place were nothing but rolling storm clouds of smoke, and spitting angry fire.

It took forever to get Cassiopeia beneath the gap. Her eyes were closed and even though her skin was hot, she was shivering so badly Lyra could barely keep ahold of her. Lyra had to repeat her name several times, and then her number, before she responded. She was passing in and out of sleep. Finally 72 had to bend down and take her by the arms, dragging her roughly free of the fence, her damaged leg twisted awkwardly behind her. She cried out in pain. This, at least, woke her up.

'What's happening?' she kept repeating, shaking. 'What's happening?'

Lyra was next. But before she could get through the fence, she heard a shout behind her. She'd been spotted. One of the guards, face invisible behind his helmet, was sprinting toward her, and she was temporarily mesmerized by the look of his gun, the enormity of it, all levers and scopes. She'd only seen the guns from a distance and didn't know why this one should be aimed at her, but for a split second she imagined the bullets screaming almost instantaneously across the distance that separated them, imagined bullets passing through layers of skin.

'Stop!' Now she could hear him. 'Stop where you are.'

Instead she dropped to her stomach and slid beneath the gap, shimmying her hips free when for a moment the bottom of the fence snagged on her pants. The guard was still shouting at her to stop but she was out, out and free and once again helping Cassiopeia to her feet. She didn't know why she was so afraid, but she was. At any second she expected to hear the chitter of bullets on the fence, feel her heart explode sideways, cleaved in two by a bullet.

But the shots didn't come, although the guard was still shouting, still coming toward them. At that second there was another rocketing blast (the fire had found its way to the storerooms in the basement of B-Wing, stocked with old chemical samples, medications, solutions marked *flammable* and *dangerous*), a final explosion that shot a plume of green flame fifty feet into the air and made the ground shudder. Cassiopeia slipped and fell backward in the mud. Lyra stumbled, and 72 caught her. For a few seconds they were inches apart, and she could smell him again, and see the fine dark line around his irises, light contracting his pupils, narrowing them to pinpoints.

From above came hailstones of granite and cement, several of them lobbing over the fence and thudding only a few feet from where they were standing. The guard had dropped to his knees and covered his head, and Lyra saw their chance. Together, she and 72 hauled Cassiopeia to her feet and went with her into the marsh. Lyra wasn't sure what they were going to do about Cassiopeia. Already she regretted taking her along. But Cassiopeia was number 6. Like Lyra, she was Gen-3, the first successful crop. Lyra had known her for as long as she could remember.

The water was warmer than she had expected, and cloudy with dirt. Banks of waist-high grass grew between stretches of thick mud and tidal pools scummy with dead insects, all of it new and strange to her, words and feelings she didn't know, sensations that tasted like blood in her mouth and panic reaching up to throttle her. Several years ago, the replicas had been woken by screaming: a man a half-mile from Spruce Island had his leg ripped off at the hip by an alligator before the guards scared it by firing into the air. He was airlifted to a nearby hospital. The nurses had for once allowed them out of their beds to watch the helicopter land with a noise like the giant whirring of insect wings, white grasses flattened by the artificial wind. Once, when she was a child, she'd even seen an alligator sunning itself on the rocky beach on the southernmost tip of the island, not four feet from the fences. She had been amazed by its knobby hide, its elongated snout, the teeth protruding jaggedly from its mouth, and she remembered standing there flooded with sudden shame: God had made that creature, that monster with a taste for blood, and loved it. But he had not made her.

She felt as if they were walking through endless tunnels bound entirely by mud and grass, and couldn't imagine that 72 knew where he was going, or where he was leading them. Cassiopeia was crying, and only the smoke still lodged in Lyra's chest, still turning the sun to a dull red ember and smudging away the sky, kept Lyra from crying, too. Haven, gone. They were outside the fence. They were in thin, unbound air, in a world of alligators and humans who hated and despised them. They were running away from safety and Lyra didn't know why. Only that the guard had come at her with a gun, looking as if he wanted to shoot.

Why had he drawn his gun? The guards were there for their own protection. To keep the outside world *out*. To keep the replicas safe.

The mosquitoes, at least, had been chased off by the smoke, although no-see-ums were still hovering in swarms over the water, and Lyra got some in her nose and mouth and even beneath her eyelids. From here, the sound of the fire was strangely musical and sounded like the steady roar of a heavy rain. But the sky was green-tinged and terrible, and the ash floated down on them.

Her arms were shaking from trying to keep Cassiopeia on her feet. Even the pillowcase felt impossibly heavy. Cassiopeia was clinging so tightly to her neck, Lyra could hardly breathe. Cassiopeia was passing in and out of consciousness, and Lyra imagined her mind like a series of ever-branching tunnels, like the marshland crisscrossed by fine veins of water, going dark and then light again.

'How much farther?' Speaking hurt.

72 just shook his head. She knew that human men were in general stronger than women and wondered whether the same thing was true of replicas. He looked strong – the muscles of his back and shoulders stood out – though he couldn't have been eating well since he escaped. She wondered where he'd gotten his food. She wondered why he'd been so desperate to get out, and whether he knew something she didn't. Or maybe he was just crazy – plenty of replicas had lost their minds before, like how Lilac Springs had lost her mind during her examinations, had forgotten all the numbers she was supposed to remember. There was Pepper, who'd used a knife to open her wrists, and number 220, who'd simply stopped eating,

and number 35, who'd started believing she was one of the rats and would only crawl on all fours. Maybe 72 was like that. Maybe he believed he was an animal and should roam free.

She couldn't go on anymore. Cassiopeia was too heavy. Every breath felt like it was hitching on a giant hook in her chest. She tried to call out to 72 but realized she didn't have the energy even for that. Instead she struggled with Cassiopeia into the reeds, finding footing on the muddy banks that stretched like fingers through the water, until the ground solidified and she could sit. 72 had to double back when he realized she was no longer behind him.

'We aren't safe here,' 72 said. He didn't sound like he'd lost his mind. She noticed how dark his eyes were, so they appeared to absorb light instead of reflecting it. 'I should leave you,' he said after a minute.

'So leave,' she said.

But he didn't. He began forcing his way through the reeds, snapping them in half with his hands when they resisted too strongly. The grass was so high and thick here it cut the sky into pieces. 'Lie down,' he instructed her, and she did. Cassiopeia was already stretched out in the mud, lips blue, eyes closed, and that sick animal smell coming off her, like the smell in the Funeral Home that no amount of detergent and bleach could conceal. Lyra could see now the glint of something metal wedged in her back, lodged deep. The muscle was visible, raw and pulsing with blood. Instinctively she brought a hand to the wound, but Cassiopeia cried out as if she'd been scalded and Lyra pulled away, her hand wet with Cassiopeia's blood. She didn't know how to make the bleeding stop. She realized she didn't know how to do anything here, in this unbound outside world. She'd never eaten except in the mess hall. She'd never slept without a nurse ordering *lights out*. She would never survive – why had she followed the male? But someone would come for her. Someone must. One of the doctors would find her and they would be saved. This was all a mistake, a terrible mistake.

Lyra squeezed her eyes shut and saw tiny explosions, silhouettes of flame drifting above Haven. She opened her eyes again. Cassiopeia moaned, and Lyra touched her forehead, as Dr. O'Donnell had once done for her. Thinking of Dr. O'Donnell made her breath hitch in her chest. There was no explanation for that feeling either – none that she knew of, anyway.

Cassiopeia moaned again.

'Shhh,' Lyra said. 'It's all right.'

'It's going to die,' 72 said flatly. Luckily, Cassiopeia didn't hear, or if she did, she was too sick to react.

'It's a she,' Lyra said.

'She's going to die, then.'

'Someone will come for us.'

'She'll die that way, too. But slower.'

'Stop,' she told him, and he shrugged and turned away. She moved a little closer to Cassiopeia. 'Want to hear a story?' she whispered. Cassiopeia didn't answer, but Lyra charged on anyway. 'Once upon a time, there was a girl named Matilda. She was really smart. Smarter than either of her parents, who were awful.' *Matilda* was one of the first long books that Dr. O'Donnell had ever read to her. She closed her eyes again and made herself focus. Once again she saw fire, but she forced the smoke into the shape of different letters, into words floating in the sky. *Extraordinary*. In the distance she heard a mechanical whirring, the sound of the air being threshed into waves: helicopters. 'Her dad was a used-car salesman. He liked to cheat people. Her mom just watched TV.' *Safe,* she thought, picturing the word pinned to clouds. 'Matilda liked to read.'

'What is that?' 72 asked, in a low voice, as if he was scared of being overheard. But he sounded angry again.

'It's a story,' she said.

'But . . .' He shook his head. She could see sand stuck to his lower lip, and dust patterning his cheekbones. 'What *is* it?'

'It's a book,' she said. 'It's called *Matilda*.' And then,

REPLICA 82 REPLICA

though she had never admitted it to anyone: 'One of the doctors read it to me.'

72 frowned again. 'You're lying,' he said, but uncertainly, as if he wasn't sure.

'I'm not,' she said. 72, she'd decided, was very ugly. His forehead was too large and his eyebrows too thick. They looked like dark caterpillars. His mouth, on the other hand, looked like a girl's. 'I have a book here. Dr. O'Donnell gave it to me. . . .' But all the breath went out of her lungs. She had reached into the pillowcase and found nothing, nothing but the file folder and the pen. The book was gone.

'I don't believe you,' 72 said. 'You don't know how to read. And the doctors would never –' He broke off suddenly, angling his head to the sky.

'I don't care whether you believe me or not,' she said. The book was gone. She was suddenly freezing. She wondered whether she should go back for it. 'I had it right here, it was *here* –'

'Quiet,' he said, holding up a hand.

'I need that book.' She felt like screaming. 'Dr. O'Donnell gave it to me so I could practice –'

But this time he brought a hand to her mouth and pulled her into him as she kicked out and shouted into his palm. She felt his warm breath against her ear.

'Please,' he whispered. The fact that he said *please*

stilled her. No one said please, not to the replicas. 'Be quiet.'

Even when she stopped struggling, he kept her pinned to him, breathing hard into her ear. She could feel his heart through her back. His hand tasted like the mud of the marshes, like salt. Sweat collected between their bodies. Insects whined.

Now the air was being segmented, cut into pulsing rhythms as if mimicking a heartbeat. The helicopters were getting closer. The sound became so loud she wanted to cover her ears. Now a wind was sweeping across the marshes, flattening the grass, driving up mud that splattered her legs and face, and just as the sound reached an unbearable crescendo she thought 72 shouted something. He leaned into her. He was on top of her, shielding her from a roar of noise and wind. And then he relaxed his hold and she saw a dozen helicopters sweep away across the marshes toward the ruins of Haven. Inside them and hanging from the open helicopter doors were helmeted men wearing drab brown-and-gray camouflage. She recognized them as soldiers. All of them had guns.

Lyra, Cassiopeia, and 72 lay in tense silence. Several helicopters went and returned. Lyra wondered whether they were bearing away the injured like they'd done for the man who'd lost his leg to an alligator, who lay screaming in the darkness while the guards lit up the water with bullets. Every time one of the helicopters passed overhead she was tempted to reveal herself, to throw up an arm or stand up out of the long grass and the knotted trees and wave. But every time, she was stopped as though by an enormous, invisible hand, frozen on the ground where she was. It was the way they churned the air to sound that made her teeth ache. It was the memory of the guard with his gun drawn, shouting at her. It was 72, lying next to her.

For a long time in the lulls they could still hear men shouting and the roar and crackle of the fire blazing on the island. Voices hung in the ashy haze, were carried by it like a bad smell. After a while, however, Lyra thought the fire must have stopped, because she could no longer hear people yelling. At the same time she realized that she could hardly see. The sky, which for hours had been the textured gray of pencil lead, was now dark. The sun was setting, and the wind when it hissed into life carried a heavy chill. The rain swept in next, the thunderstorms that always came in the early evening, quick and ferocious, punching down on them. By the time it had passed, the sun was gone.

Cassiopeia was completely still. Lyra was afraid to touch her and find she was dead, but when she did she felt a pulse. Periodically the sky was lit up with helicopters passing back and forth, and every so often, a shout carried over the water. Lyra thought of her small clean bed under the third window in the dorm and had to swallow back the urge to cry again. She wouldn't have thought she could be so cold, and so afraid, and also have to fight so hard against sleep. At some point she must have drifted off because she woke from a nightmare of monsters with long metal snouts, and felt 72 put a hand against her mouth again, and lean his weight against her to speak into her ear.

'They're searching the marshes,' 72 whispered. 'Stay quiet. Don't move. Don't even breathe.'

Her heart was still racing from the nightmare. It was so dark, she could hardly make out Cassiopeia lying even a few feet away. But after a second she saw light flashing through the tall grass, tiny suns blazing and being drowned. She heard voices, too – not the panicked and indistinct shouting of earlier but individual voices and words.

'Over here. That's blood, boys.'

'Christ. Like a slug trail.'

'You bring any salt . . . ?'

She was afraid. Why was she afraid? She didn't know. She wasn't thinking clearly. The guards were on her side. They had kept the others out – they kept the replicas safe. But still fear had its hand down her throat. This was her chance to change her mind, to call out, to be rescued. 72 shifted next to her, and she stayed silent.

'Here's one.' One of the men raised the cry and lights flashed again, dazzling over the dark water, as several other soldiers joined him where he stood. She wanted so badly to look – but even as she started to raise herself onto her elbow, 72 jerked her back to the ground.

'Stay put,' he whispered. She heard laughter from the soldiers, more words half blown by wind.

'Bring a – ?'

'No point . . . dead . . .'

'No bodies . . . left . . .'

'It looks real, doesn't it?'

Lyra was filled with a cold so deep it felt like a pit. *It looks real, doesn't it?* She knew they'd found another replica – a dead one – and wondered what she would look like to them if they came across her with their flashlights: like something mechanical, a machine, or like a doll with moving parts. She imagined herself like a jigsaw puzzle – she had seen one, once, in the nurses' break room – well-crafted, neatly jointed, but full of seams and cracks visible to everyone else. She wondered whether humans had some invisible quality, the truly critical one, she'd never be able to replicate.

They were coming closer, slowing through the water. Now she couldn't have cried out even if she wanted to.

Her lungs had seized in her chest. She had to grind her teeth to keep them from chattering.

'More blood over here, see?'

Lyra's heart stopped. The men were just on the other side of the embankment. Their flashlights slanted through the grass – were they well enough concealed? Would they be seen?

'Keep an eye out for gators. These marshes are crawling.'

'Maybe we should give Johnson up for bait.'

More laughter. Lyra squeezed her eyes shut. *Move on,* she thought, still uncertain whether this was the right thing. All she knew was that she didn't want them to see her. They couldn't see her. *Move on.*

Then there was a horrible sucking, gasping noise, like water fighting through a stuck drain. For one confused second, Lyra couldn't tell where it was coming from. Then she realized Cassiopeia was trying to speak.

'Help.' The word was mangled, distorted by the sound of liquid in her lungs.

'No, Cassiopeia,' Lyra whispered, dizzy now with panic. But already she knew it was too late. The soldiers had gone silent.

Cassiopeia spoke a little louder. 'Help.'

'In here.' One of the men was already crashing through the trees toward them, and the marshes were once again alive with lights and shouting. 'There's someone in here.'

'Leave her. *Leave* her.' 72's voice, when he whispered, was raw with panic. This time Lyra didn't resist, didn't even argue. 72 was going elbow over elbow into the tangle of growth. She crawled after him as fast as she could on her stomach. The ground trembled under the weight of the soldiers' boots as she fought deeper into the growth. Pine needles grabbed her face and arms and scored tiny cuts in her skin. She was too scared to look back. She was certain they would be heard, crashing through the grass, but the soldiers were loud, calling to one another in a rapid patter she didn't understand.

Then the trees released them into a heavy slick of puddled mud and water: they'd reached another sudden opening in the land, a place where the marsh became liquid. 72 slid into the water first and Lyra pulled herself in next to him just as a beam of light swept over the bank where she'd been. She slipped down to her chin, gasping a little, certain they must have heard her, and then submerged herself to her eyes. The beam of the light continued sniffing along the mud like something alive. Twelve inches from her, then ten . . .

'There's a trail here,' one of the men called out, crashing through the growth, kicking aside the spindly branches lit up by his flashlight. Lyra knew they were finished. 'Looks like something crawled out this way.'

The light inched closer, touching the water now, so close to her nose she drew back. . . .

'Found it.'

The light froze where it was. If it had truly been an animal it would have been close enough to lick her. Then the soldier on the bank turned and retreated in the other direction.

'Dead or alive?'

'What the fuck, alive.'

'Doesn't look like it.'

How many were there? Three? Four? It was so hard to tell. How many were out there in the marshes with their lights and boots and heavy guns?

Cassiopeia spoke up one more time, faintly now. 'Help me.'

'Awww, Jesus Christ. There's blood all over the place. It got a bullet in the back or something.'

'Might as well put a bullet in the front, too. No way it's gonna make it all the way to base.'

'Are you kidding? You know how expensive these things are to make? Might as well take a dump on a hundred grand.'

Beneath the surface, something slick and heavy brushed Lyra's arm, and she stifled a scream. She wondered if even now there were alligators circling them in the dark, or snakes with sleek black bodies and poisonous fangs. High above them the stars glittered coldly in a perfectly clear sky.

'Damn it. All right then. On three?'

'You're kidding, right? It's bleeding. That's how it spreads.'

'Not unless you eat them, you dumb shit. What's the matter? You hungry?'

More laughter. There were definitely three of them. At least three. For the first time in her life, something black and deep and hateful stretched out of Lyra's stomach. She hated them. She hated that they could laugh and that they were afraid to touch Cassiopeia. She hated their easy way of talking. She hated that she could look like a human, and yet she was not a human, and they could tell.

But just as quickly as it had come, the hatred passed. She was cold and tired and scared. She had no energy to be angry, too.

At least the soldiers were going, and leaving Cassiopeia behind after all.

'It's already dead,' one of them said. 'See? Let one of the cleanup crews get to it tomorrow.' There was the sound of a boot against a body, several hard thumps. Lyra sank down another inch in the water, as if she could flood the sound from her ears.

If there were alligators in the water, they could chew off her feet and she wouldn't notice . . . or maybe her feet were already gone, maybe the pain had numbed her . . . the idea was so awful it struck her as funny. She might be standing there on two stumps, bleeding out into the swamp like Cassiopeia.

'It's all right. They're gone now.' In the darkness 72's features were softened. Then she realized she'd been laughing out loud, laughing and shivering. The men were gone. The marshes were silent and still except for another helicopter that took off in the distance and swept out toward Barrel Key. She waded out of the water after him, slipping on the mud.

'What if they come back?' she asked, through the hard freeze in her chest. She knew it couldn't really be cold. 72 didn't seem cold at all, and the nurses had been complaining only yesterday about the awful heat. The cold must have somehow been inside, lodged in her chest like the piece of metal that got Cassiopeia in the back. She wanted to go and look at Cassiopeia, to make sure she was really dead. But she was so tired.

'They won't be back,' he said. 'They'll finish searching the marshes, but they won't come back, not for a while at least. Lie down,' he said, and she did, so tired that she didn't even pull away when he lay down next to her. Already she was half-asleep, drowning in a tangled liquid dream. But when he put his arms around her, she jerked briefly awake.

'The human body,' he said, without letting go of her, his voice low and sleepy, 'is full of nerve cells.'

'I know,' she said, reassured, 'ten trillion of them.'

She was asleep again, and dreaming of ten trillion nerves lighting up like stars against a bloodred, pulsing sky.

NINE

SHE WOKE UP WARM, SWEATING, from a dream she couldn't remember. The smell of smoke was fainter now. Her cheek was crusty with mud. The shock of what had happened had passed. She knew immediately where she was but not what had woken her. But something *had* woken her.

She sat up, wondering what time it was. Her body ached. She knew from the darkness it must still be the middle of the night. Beside her, 72 was sleeping with both hands folded beneath his head and his mouth open. He looked much younger when he slept.

Even before she heard a footstep she knew that someone was nearby and that this, the sound of someone close, was what had woken her. She took hold of 72's arm, and he came awake at the same time she heard a girl speak.

'What now?' she said. 'Do you think we can still

get – ?' But she abruptly fell silent, and Lyra realized she had made a sound without meaning to.

They must be more soldiers sent to comb the marshes. And yet the girl didn't speak like a soldier, and wasn't moving like one, either, with a fearlessness born from their guns. These people – she had no doubt they were people, and not replicas – were doing their best to stay quiet. Almost as if they, too, were afraid of being seen.

Who were they? What did they want?

72 was alert now, listening. The people – whoever they were – seemed to be just on the other side of the misshapen trees that grew all through the marshes; Nurse Don't-Even-Think-About-It had said they were bad luck. Lyra and 72 had to move. She shifted into a crouch, and a twig snapped beneath her weight.

'Don't move,' 72 whispered. 'Don't move.'

But it was too late. She heard crashing in the brush. In the darkness all the sounds were confused, and she didn't know what had happened and whether they'd been found.

'Who's there?' 72 called out. But no one answered.

Lyra stood up and plunged blindly in one direction, sliding a little on the mud, her own breath harsh and alien-sounding. Pain ripped through her heel where she stepped: the marshes were full of toothy things, plants and animals that bit back, a world of things that only wanted to draw blood, and for a second she was aware of the stars infinitely high above her, the distance and coldness of them, a long dark plunge into emptiness. There was nowhere to go, nowhere to run. In the world outside Haven she was nothing, had no past and no future.

Shadows moved on her left. Something heavy hit the ground, and the girl cried out.

Lyra froze. She'd run in exactly the wrong direction, straight toward the strangers and not away from them.

'Jesus. Jesus Christ.'

'That voice.' The girl spoke again. 'Where did it come from?'

'I don't know. Christ, Gemma. *Look . . .*'

Lyra heard coughing, as if someone was trying not to throw up. This, the evidence of side effects, calmed her. Maybe she'd been wrong. Maybe these were replicas who'd somehow escaped the way she did. She inched forward, parting the tangle of grasses with a hand, until she saw a boy silhouetted in the moonlight, his hand to his mouth, and the girl crouching beside him, whimpering.

'What the hell? What the hell?' he kept saying.

The moon broke loose of the clouds and clarified their features. Forgetting to be afraid, Lyra went forward.

'Cassiopeia,' she said, because she was confused, still half in shock. Of course the girl couldn't be Cassiopeia, just like it couldn't be any of her genotypes, 7–10:

Cassiopeia was dead, and her genotypes didn't have soft brown hair, soft *everything*, a pretty roundness to their faces and bodies. Lyra stopped again, seeing in the grass next to the girl the body, the slender ankles and familiar wristband, the blood darkening her shirt. Cassiopeia. And yet the girl crouching next to her had Cassiopeia's face and round little nose and freckles. A genotype, then, like Calliope and Goosedown and Tide and Charmin, but one that Lyra didn't know. Were replicas made in other places, too? It was the only thing she could think of that made sense.

The boy stumbled backward, as if he was afraid Lyra might attack him. The girl – Cassiopeia's replica, identical to her except for the extra weight she carried and the hair that grazed her shoulders – was staring at Lyra, mouth open as though she was trying to scream but couldn't.

Finally Cassiopeia's replica said, 'Oh my God. I think – I think she's one of them.'

'Who are you?' Lyra managed to say. 'Where did you come from?'

'Who are *you*?' The boy had a nice face, geometric, and she found it easy to look at him.

'Lyra,' she said, because she decided there was no point in lying. 'Number twenty-four,' she clarified, because wherever they came from, they must have number systems, too. But they just stared at her blankly. She couldn't understand it. She felt as she had when she had first started to read, staring at the cipher of the letters, those spiky evil things that kept their meaning locked away.

'Oh my God.' The girl brought a hand to her mouth. 'There's another one.'

Lyra turned and saw 72 edging out into the open, holding a knife. He must have stolen it from the kitchen before escaping, and she doubted it was very sharp, but the strangers didn't know that. Now the boy had both hands out. Lyra thought he looked nervous. For a split second he reminded her of the nurses, and the narrow way they looked at the replicas, and she almost hoped that 72 would hurt him.

'Look,' he said. He wet his bottom lip with his tongue. 'Hold on a second. Just hold on.'

'Who are you?' 72 came to stand next to Lyra. She couldn't tell what he was thinking. His face, so open in sleep, had closed again, and she had never learned how to read other people's moods and feelings, had never been taught to.

'We're nobody,' the boy said. Slowly he helped the girl to her feet. She was wearing normal clothing, Lyra noticed. People-clothing. She understood less than ever. 'Listen, we're not going to hurt you, okay? My name's Jake Witz. This is Gemma. We got lost in the marshes, that's all.'

Lyra was now more confused than ever. 'But . . .' She met the girl's eyes for the first time. It was hard to look at her with Cassiopeia, poor Cassiopeia, lying dead at her feet between them. Who would come to collect her body? Who would bundle her up for burning? 'Who made you?'

'What?' the girl whispered.

'Who made you?' Lyra repeated. She'd never heard of other places like Haven, and she felt a small stirring of hope, as if a heavy locked door in her chest had just been unlatched. Maybe there were places for them to go after all, places where there were people to take care of them like they'd been cared for at Haven, places with high walls to keep everyone else out.

'I – I don't understand,' the girl said. Her eyes were so wide Lyra could see a whole portion of the night sky reflected in them.

'You're a replica,' Lyra said impatiently. The girl was slow, much slower than Cassiopeia. But she knew that this wasn't uncommon. She thought of Lilac Springs – dead now, probably. And 101, who'd never even learned how to hold a fork. She wondered how many of the others had burned.

'A what?' the girl whispered.

'A replica,' Lyra repeated. The girl shook her head. Where she came from, they must be called something different. She recited, 'An organism descended from or genetically identical to a single common ancestor.'

'A clone,' the girl said, staring at Lyra so fixedly she was reminded of being under the observation lights, and looked away. 'She means a *clone*, Jake.'

'Yeah, well. I kind of already had that impression,' the boy said, and he made a face, as if he was offended by the sight of Cassiopeia's body.

Lyra had the sudden urge to reach down and close Cassiopeia's eyes and wasn't sure where it had come from – maybe something one of the nurses had said about the way people buried one another. In Haven, the dead replicas had always simply been burned or dumped.

'But – but it's impossible.' The girl's voice had gotten very shrill. 'It's impossible, the technology doesn't exist, it's *illegal*. . . .'

Lyra lost patience. The girl was either suffering from side effects or she was very, very stupid to begin with. *Failure to thrive.* 'It's not impossible,' she said. 'At Haven, there were thousands of replicas.'

'Jesus.' The boy closed his eyes. His face was like a second moon, pale and glowing. 'Clones. It all makes sense now. . . .'

'Are you crazy? *Nothing* makes sense.' The girl had turned away, covering her mouth with her hand again, as if she was trying to force back the urge to be sick. 'There's a *dead girl* with *my face* on her. We're standing here in the middle of the fucking night and these – these people are telling me that there are clones running around out there, thousands of them –'

'Gemma, calm down. Okay? Everyone needs to calm down.' The boy spoke loudly even though the girl was the only one who wasn't calm, or the only one who was showing it, at least. 'Can you put that thing down, please?' This was to 72, still holding the knife. 'We're not going to hurt you.'

Suddenly Lyra was hit with a wave of dizziness. She went into a crouch and put her head between her knees. Her head was full of a hot and sticky darkness, a swirling that reminded her of heavy clouds of circulating gnats.

'What's the matter with her?' She heard the girl's voice, but distantly. If 72 responded, she didn't hear him.

'Hey.' A minute later, the girl was next to her. 'Are you okay?' She put a hand on Lyra's back, and Lyra jerked away. She was used to being touched, manipulated, even opened up with knives and needles; but this felt different, intimate and almost shameful, like when she'd first been caught by Nurse-Don't-Even-Think-About-It in the bathroom with her hands submerged in bleach, trying to scrub her first period blood from her underwear. She couldn't speak. She was afraid that if she opened her mouth, she would throw up. The girl stood up again and moved away from her, and Lyra almost regretted jerking away. But she didn't want to be touched by strangers, not anymore, not if she could help it.

Except – she remembered falling asleep, exhausted, on the ground, the way the stars had blurred into a single bright point, leading her into sleep – she hadn't minded when 72 put his arms around her for warmth. But she was in shock, exhausted. She had needed the body heat. The world outside was too big: it was nice to feel bounded by something.

'Maybe she's hungry,' the boy said.

She wasn't hungry, but she stayed quiet. The worst of the nausea had released her, though. Strange how it came like that in dizzying rushes, like getting hit in the head. She sat back, too exhausted to stand again. She was no longer afraid, either. It was obvious that the strangers weren't there to hurt them or to take them anywhere. Now she just wished they would move on. She didn't understand the girl who was a replica but didn't know it. She didn't understand the boy who was with her, and how they were related.

72 took a quick step forward. 'You have food?'

The boy looked to Cassiopeia's genotype, and she made a quick, impatient gesture with her hand. He shrugged out of his backpack and squatted to unzip it. Lyra had never had the chance to observe two males so close together, and noticed he moved differently from 72. His movements were slow, as if his whole body hurt. 72 moved with a quickness that seemed like an attack. 'Sorry. We didn't bring much.'

72 came forward cautiously. He snatched up a granola bar and a bottle of water and then backtracked quickly. 72 tore open the granola bar with his teeth, spitting out the wrapper, and began to eat. He kept his eyes on the boy – Jake – the whole time, and Lyra knew that he was worried the boy might try to take it back from him. But Jake only watched him.

72 opened the water, drank half of it, and then passed it to Lyra without removing his eyes from Jake. 'Drink,' he said. 'You'll feel better.'

She hadn't realized how raw her throat felt until she drank, washing away some of the taste of ash and burning. She wished that Jake and Cassiopeia's replica would leave so that she could go back to sleep. At the same time, she was worried about what the morning would bring when they found themselves alone on the marshes again, with no food, nothing to drink, nowhere to go.

'Look.' The boy was talking to Lyra. Maybe he'd decided she was easier to talk to. Maybe he hadn't forgotten that 72 had a knife. 'I know you must be tired – you've been through – I don't even *know* what you've been through . . .'

'Jake . . .' Cassiopeia's replica pressed her hand to her eyes.

'They've been living in Haven, Gemma,' the boy said quickly. 'My father died for this. I need to know.'

Father. The word sent a curious tremor up Lyra's spine, as if she'd been tapped between her vertebrae. So Lyra was right about him: he was natural-born.

'Jake, *no.*' Cassiopeia's replica – the boy had said her name was Gemma, Lyra remembered now – looked and sounded like one of the nurses. Jake fell silent. 'I don't believe you,' she said. 'I literally don't believe you. These poor people have been through God knows what – they're starving and cold and they have no place to go – and you want to *interview* them –'

'I don't want to interview them. I want to understand.'

Lyra took another sip of water, swallowing despite the pain. 'Not people,' she said, because the girl had been nice to them and she thought it was worth correcting her.

Gemma turned to stare at Lyra. 'What?'

'We're not people,' Lyra said. 'You said, "These poor people have been through god knows what." But we're replicas. God didn't make us. Dr. Saperstein did. He's *our* god.' She stopped herself from pointing out that Gemma, too, must have been made by someone, even if she didn't know it.

Gemma kept staring, until Lyra finally felt uncomfortable and looked down at her hands. Had she said the wrong thing again? But she was just reciting what she knew to be true, what everyone had always told her.

Finally Gemma spoke again. Her voice was much softer now. 'We should camp here for the night,' she said. For an instant, she even sounded like Dr. O'Donnell. 'We'll go back to Wahlee in the morning.'

'We're not going anywhere with you,' 72 said quickly. Lyra was surprised to hear him say *we*. She had never been a *we*. Maybe he'd only confused the word, the way she still confused *I* and *it* sometimes.

'No,' Gemma said. 'No, you don't have to go with us. Not unless you want to.'

'Why would we want to?' 72 asked. In the dark he was all hard angles, like someone hacked out of shadow. Now Lyra wasn't sure whether he was ugly or not. His face kept changing, and every time the light fell on it differently he looked like a new person.

Cassiopeia's replica didn't blink. 'You can't plan on staying here forever. You have no money. No ID. You're not even supposed to exist. And there will be people looking for you.'

The girl was right. *You're not even supposed to exist.* Lyra knew the truth of these words, even though she wasn't sure exactly what they meant. Hadn't that been the point of the guards and the fences? To keep the replicas safe, and secret, and protected? Everyone who had known them had despised them. *You're not supposed to exist.* Wasn't that what the nurses were always saying? That they were monsters and abominations? All except Nurse Em, all those years ago, and Dr. O'Donnell. But both of them had gone away.

Everyone went away, in the end.

'Can I have more water?' she asked, and so somehow it was decided. 72 turned to look at her with an expression she couldn't read, but she was too tired to worry about him and what he thought and whether they were making the right decision.

Neither of the strangers wanted to sleep near Cassiopeia's body, so they moved instead through the thick patch of hobble-backed trees and tall grasses streaked with bird guano, leaving the corpse behind. Lyra didn't understand it. She liked being near to Cassiopeia's body. It was comforting. She could imagine she was back at Haven, even, that she and Cassiopeia were just lying in separate cots across the narrow space that divided them.

Gemma, the girl, suggested she try a soda. Lyra had never had soda before. At Haven, the vending machines were for the staff only, although sometimes the nurses took pity on the younger replicas and gave them coins from the vending machines to play with, to roll or flip or barter. Her first impression was that it was much, much too sweet. But she felt better after a few sips, less nauseous. Her hands were steadier, too.

Gemma found a clean sweatshirt in the bottom of Jake's bag and offered it to 72, but he refused. So instead Lyra took it, though it was far too big and she did nothing but pull it on over the filth of her regular shirt. She was warm now, but she was also comforted by the feel of clean cotton and the smell of it, like the laundry detergent they used at Haven that sent the sheets back stiff and crisp as paper. This sweatshirt wasn't stiff, but soft, so soft.

She curled up on the ground and 72 sat next to her.

'I don't trust them,' he whispered, looking over to where the boy and girl were making camp, arguing over who should be allowed to use the backpack as a pillow. 'They're not like us.'

'No,' she said. Her tongue felt thick. Her mind felt thick, too, as if it had also been blanketed in cotton. She wanted to say: *We don't exist.* She wanted to say: *We have no choice.* But even as she reached for the words, the cord tethering her thoughts snapped, and she was bobbing, wordless, mindless, into the dark.

It seemed she'd barely fallen asleep before she was jerked into awareness again by movement beside her. She sat up and saw 72 half on his feet with the knife in his hand.

The girl Gemma was standing above them, and for a confused second, before the clutch of dream fully released her, Lyra again mistook her for Cassiopeia and felt a leap of feeling she had no name for.

'It's okay,' the girl said. 'It's just me. Gemma, remember?'

72 lowered his knife. Lyra thought he must have been having a bad dream. He looked pale. They'd woken up very close together, side by side again. She wondered whether he'd reached for her again in the middle of the night. For body heat. A person's average body temperature fell during sleep, she knew, sometimes by a full degree. Another thing she had heard and remembered.

'There are still men on the island,' Gemma said immediately. 'They're burning what's left of Haven.'

'You saw them? You got close?' The other one, Jake, had woken, too. He stood up, shoving a hand through his hair. Lyra had always been fascinated by hair – she and the other replicas had their scalps shaved every week – and was temporarily mesmerized by the way it fell. 'You should have woken me. It's not safe.'

Lyra barely heard him. She stood, too, despite the fact that her legs felt gelatinous and uncertain. The sky was getting light. 'What do you mean, they're burning what's left of Haven?'

'Just what I said,' Gemma said.

Lyra had a sudden explosion of memories: the smell of the Stew Pot in the morning and the way the sunlight patterned the linoleum; the courtyard paths splotched with guano; the medicinal smell of a swab on her arm, the pinch of a needle, a voice murmuring she would be okay, okay. All her friends, Squeezeme and Thermoscan and even the Glass Eyes, who could never entirely be trusted – all of them gone. Lyra's memories felt right then like physical things, punching up into her consciousness. The small cot with her number fixed to the steel headboard. Showerheads arrayed in a row and the smell of soap-scented steam and the echo of dozens of voices. Laundry day and trash day and the mournful bellow of the departing barges. Even the things she hated: paper cups filled with pills and vitamins, the nurses sneering at the replicas, or worse, acting as though they were afraid.

Still. Haven was home. It was where she belonged.

'Then there's no going back?' She hadn't realized, fully realized, until the words were out of her mouth that on some level she had been holding on to the idea that this would all pass – the explosions and the fire and the soldiers shouting *stop,* saying, *You know how expensive these things are to make?* – all of it would be explained. Then they would be herded up, they would be returned to Haven, 72 included. They would be evaluated by doctors. The nurses would distribute pills: the prim white Hush-Hush for pain, the slightly larger Sleepers that made the world relax into fog. Everything would return to normal.

'There's no going back,' 72 said. He wasn't as hard with her as he'd been the day before. Lyra wondered if it was because he felt sorry for her. 'I told you that. They'll kill us if they find us. One way or another, they'll kill us.'

Lyra turned away. She wouldn't listen. The guards and soldiers were trained to kill. And she had never liked the doctors or the nurses, the researchers or the birthers with their incomprehensible speech. But she knew that Haven had existed to protect them, that the doctors were trying to keep them safe against the cancers that exploded through the tissue of their lungs and livers and brains, against the diseases that reversed the normal processes of life and made food go up instead of down or lungs drown in fluid of their own creation.

Side effects. The replication process was still imperfect. If it weren't for the doctors, Lyra and 72 would have died years ago, as infants, like so many replicas had, like the whole yellow crop did. She remembered all those tiny bodies bundled carefully in paper sheaths, each of them no bigger than a loaf of bread. Hundreds of them borne away on the barge to be burned in the middle of the ocean.

'We have to get off the marshes. There will be new patrols now that it's light. They'll be looking for survivors.'

Gemma was speaking in a low voice, the kind of voice Lyra associated with the nurses when they wanted something: *calm down, deep breath, just a little burn.* 'Come with us, and we'll get you clothes, and hide you someplace no one will be looking for you. Then you can figure out where to go. *We* can figure it out.'

'Okay,' Lyra said, because 72 had just opened his mouth, and she was tired of being spoken for, tired of letting him decide for her. He wasn't a doctor. He had no right to tell her what to do. But she had followed him and she had to make the best of it.

Besides, she didn't think Gemma wanted to hurt them, though she couldn't have said why. Maybe only because Gemma was Cassiopeia's replica, although she knew that was stupid – genotypes often had different personalities. Number 120 had tried to suffocate her own genotype while she slept, because she wanted to be the real one. The only one. Cassiopeia was nice to Lyra, but Calliope liked to kill things. She had once killed a bird while Lyra was watching. And 121 had never spoken a single word.

'Okay, we'll go with you,' she said a little louder, when 72 turned to look at her. She was pleased when he didn't argue, felt a little stronger, a little more in control. Cassiopeia's replica would help them. They needed to know what had happened to Haven and why. Then they could figure out what to do next.

Jake and Gemma had come on a boat called a kayak. Lyra had never seen one before and didn't especially want to ride in it, but there was no choice. Gemma and Jake would have to go on foot, and there might be places so deep they'd have to swim. Neither 72 nor Lyra had ever learned to swim, and she nearly asked him what he had meant by trying to escape Haven, how he'd expected to survive. When she was little she had sometimes dreamed of escape, dreamed of going home on the launches with one of the staff members, being dressed and cared for and cuddled. But she had learned better, had folded that need down inside of her, stored it away. Otherwise, she knew, she might go crazy, like so many of the other replicas who'd chosen to die or tried to sneak out on the trash barges with the nurses and been killed by exhaust in the engine room.

Once again, she wondered if 72 was just a little bit crazy.

Being in the kayak felt like being on a narrow, extremely wobbly gurney. The seat was wet. Her stomach lurched as 72 shoved the kayak into the shallows and then clambered in himself, refusing Jake's help. She couldn't believe they didn't just sink. She was uncomfortably aware of the sloshing of the water below her, which seemed to be attempting to jettison her out of her seat. She was afraid to move, afraid even to breathe.

But miraculously, the kayak stayed afloat, and 72 soon got the hang of paddling. The muscles in his arms and shoulders stood out when he moved, and Lyra found him unexpectedly beautiful to watch. She began to relax, despite the painful slowness of their progress and the continued rhythm of motorboats in the distance, and the ripples from their wakes that sent water sloshing into the kayak.

She should be afraid. She didn't know much about feelings, but she knew that Gemma was afraid, and Jake was afraid, and even 72 was afraid. But for some reason, for a short time, the fear released her. She was floating, gliding toward a new life. She had never thought she'd know what it felt like to be out on the water, had never imagined that a life outside Haven could exist. The outside world, constantly visible to her through the fence, had nonetheless seemed like the soap operas she sometimes saw on the nurses' TV: pretty to look at but essentially unreal.

But the novelty soon wore off. The insects were thick. Gnats swarmed them in mists. They hardly seemed to be moving. Tendrils of floating grass made certain routes impassable and had to be manually separated or threshed aside with a paddle. Several times Gemma lost her footing in the water and nearly went under. Lyra wondered how long they would be able to go, whether they would make it. She wondered whether they would have to leave Gemma behind, and thought of Cassiopeia lying in the reeds while the sun burned away her retinas.

She felt a momentary regret but didn't know why. Death was natural. Decay, too. It was another thing that made replicas and humans similar: they died.

Finally Gemma called them to a stop. Lyra was relieved for the break and the chance to get off the water, especially now that the midmorning sun was like an exposed eye.

They'd barely dragged the kayak out of the water when Jake yelled, 'Get down.'

The hum of an approaching helicopter suddenly doubled, tripled in volume. Lyra's breath was knocked away by its pressure. They went into a crouch beneath the fat sprawl of a mangrove tree as the helicopter roared by overhead. The whole ground trembled. Marsh grass lay flat beneath the wind threshed from the helicopter's giant rotor. Looking up through the branches, Lyra saw a soldier leaning out of the open door to point at something on the horizon. Then the helicopter was gone.

They left the kayak behind and went the rest of the way on foot. The ground was soft and wet and they had to wade through tidal pools where the mud was studded with sharp-toothed clams and splinters of broken shells. The growth here was different, the trees taller and less familiar to Lyra. She felt as if they were moving deep in an undiscovered wilderness and was shocked when instead Gemma gave a cry of relief and the trees opened up to reveal a small dirt clearing, corroded metal trash bins, and various signs she was too tired to read.

'Thank God,' Gemma said. Lyra watched as Jake moved to a dusty car parked in the lot and loaded his backpack into it. She was afraid all over again. She knew about cars because she'd seen them on TV and Lazy Ass was always complaining about hers, *piece-of-shit*, but she didn't think she wanted to ride in one. Especially since, according to Lazy Ass's stories, at least, cars were always breaking down or leaking oil or giving trouble in some way.

But once again, they had no choice. And at the very least, being in the car felt better, sturdier, than being in the kayak, although as soon as Jake began bumping down the road, Lyra had to close her eyes to keep from being sick. But this only made things worse. The car was louder, too, than she'd thought it would be. The windows rattled and the engine sounded like a wild animal and the radio was so loud Lyra thought her head would explode. They were going so fast that the outside world looked blurry, and she had to close her eyes again.

To calm herself she recited the alphabet in her head, then counted up from one to one hundred. She listed

LYRA

115

GEMMA

all the constellations she knew, but that was painful: she imagined Cassiopeia's face, and Ursa Major's obsession with hoarding things from the mess hall – old spoons and paper cups, bags of oyster crackers and packages of mustard – and wondered whether she would ever see any of the other replicas again.

'Hey. Are you all right? It's okay – we're stopped now.'

Lyra opened her eyes and saw that Gemma was right: they had stopped. They were in what looked like an enormous loading dock, but filled with dozens and dozens of parked cars instead of boats – *a parking lot*, another idea she'd absorbed from the nurses without ever having seen it. Could all the cars belong to different people? Looming in the distance was a building three times the size of even the Box. W-A-L-M-A-R-T. Lyra flexed her fingers, which ached. She had been holding tight to her seat without realizing it.

'You guys can stay here, okay?' Gemma said. 'Just sit tight. We're going to buy food and stuff. And clothes,' she added. 'Do you know your shoe size?'

Lyra shook her head. At Haven they were provided with sandals or slippers. Sometimes they were too big, other times too small, but Lyra so often went barefoot she hadn't thought it mattered.

'Okay.' Gemma exhaled. 'What did you say your names were again?'

'I'm Lyra,' Lyra said. 'And this is seventy-two.' She was distracted. Outside the car, Jake was speaking on a cell phone. Lyra felt a twinge of nervousness. Who was he calling? Every so often, he glanced back into the car as if to make sure that Lyra and 72 were still there. What if 72 was right, and Jake and Gemma couldn't be trusted?

'Seventy-two?' Gemma repeated. 'That isn't a name.'

'It's my number,' 72 said shortly.

'I'm twenty-four,' Lyra said, by way of explanation. 'But one of the doctors named me.' 72 looked faintly annoyed, but Lyra knew he was probably just jealous, because he didn't yet have a name.

'Wow,' Jake said. 'And I thought being named after my father was bad. Sorry,' he added quickly. 'Dumb joke. Just . . . stay here, okay? We'll be back in ten minutes.'

For a while, 72 and Lyra sat in silence. Lyra figured out how to roll down the window but found no relief from the heat outside. It was what Nurse Don't-Even-Think-About-It had called molasses-hot. She watched Jake and Gemma as they narrowed into brushstrokes and then disappeared into W-A-L-M-A-R-T. Gemma's reference to a grandmother bothered her — but it excited her, too, because of what it meant.

Finally she said, 'I don't think the girl knows she's a replica.'

72 had been staring out the window — fists lodged in

his armpits, hunched over as though he were cold, which was impossible. He turned to her. 'What?'

'The girl's a replica. But I don't think she knows it.' The idea was taking shape now, and with it the simple suggestion of possibility, of a life that might exist on the other side of Haven. At the same time, she was afraid to voice the possibility out loud, aware that it would sound silly and afraid of what 72 would say. 'Which means . . . well, maybe she comes from a place where being a replica doesn't make a difference. Where they have families and drive cars and things like that.'

Lyra could see herself reflected in 72's eyes. They were the color of the maple syrup served in the Stew Pot on special occasions, like Christmas and the anniversary of the first God's death. 'Is that what you want?' he said at last. 'You want a family?'

'I don't know.' Lyra turned away from him, embarrassed by the intensity of his stare, which felt like being back in the Box, like being evaluated, having her eyes and knees tested for reflexes. Her idea of *mother* looked much like the nurses and the Haven staff. Mother was someone to feed and clothe you and make sure you took your medicines. But now, unbidden, an image of Dr. O'Donnell came to her. She imagined herself tucked up in a big white bed while Dr. O'Donnell read out loud. She remembered the way that Dr. O'Donnell's hands had smelled, and the feel of fingertips skimming the crown of her head. *Good night, Lyra.* And there were her dreams, too, impressions of a birther who held and rocked her, and a cup with lions around its rim. When she was younger she had searched the mess hall for such a cup before being forced to admit that all the glasses at Haven were plain, made of clear plastic. She knew her dreams must be just that – dreams, a kind of wishful thinking.

But she was too ashamed to confess what she was thinking: that she could find Dr. O'Donnell. That Dr. O'Donnell could be her mother. 'What do you want?' Lyra asked instead, turning to 72. 'You ran away, even if you didn't get far.'

'I couldn't,' 72 said. 'I couldn't figure out a way past the guards.'

'You must have been hoping that something like this would happen,' Lyra said, and a suspicion flickered: Could 72 have somehow been responsible for the disaster at Haven? But no. That didn't make any sense. They were standing together when the explosion happened. They were touching.

72 frowned as if he knew what she was thinking. 'I didn't hope for anything,' he said. 'I was just waiting for my chance.'

'But you must have had a plan,' she insisted. 'You

must have had an idea of where you would go on the other side.'

'I didn't have a plan.' He leaned back, closing his eyes. As soon as he did, he once again looked much younger. Or not younger, exactly. Stripped down, somehow, naked. Lyra remembered that once she and Ursa Major and Cassiopeia had spied on the males' dormitory from the courtyard. Through a partially open blind they'd seen the blurry and bony silhouette of one of the males shirtless and they'd stumbled backward, shocked and gasping, when he turned in their direction. Looking at 72 gave Lyra the same feeling of peering through those blinds, and left her excited and also terrified.

She was almost relieved when he opened his eyes again.

'You asked me what I want. I'll tell you what I don't want. I don't want to spend the rest of my life being told what to do, and what to eat, and when to sleep, and when to use the bathroom. I'm tired of being a lab rat.'

'What do you mean, *a lab rat*?' It was so hot, Lyra was having trouble thinking. Once or twice she'd been sent into B-Wing for some reason or another and seen the milk-white rats in their cages, had seen when they threaded their paws through the bars the elongated pinkness of their strangely human fingers. And some of them were suffering in some stage of an experiment, bloated with pain or covered in dozens of tumorous growths, so heavy they couldn't lift their heads.

'I watched,' he said simply. 'I paid attention.' He turned his face to the window. 'When I was little, I didn't know the difference. I thought I might be an animal. I thought I must be.'

Lyra had an uncomfortable memory again, of number 35 crawling on all fours, insisting on eating her dinner from a bowl on the ground. But number 35 had been soft in the brain. Everyone said so.

'Aren't you worried about what will happen?' she asked. 'Without medicine, without check-ins, with no one to help us when we get sick? We weren't *made* for the outside.'

But even as she said it, Lyra thought again of Dr. O'Donnell. She *knew* how the replicas were built. She was a doctor and she'd worked at Haven. She could help.

'You really believe.' It wasn't a question. He had turned back to her. 'You believe everything they ever told you.'

'What do you mean?' she asked. It was so hot. Her face was hot. He was looking at her like some of the nurses did, like she wasn't exactly real, like he was struggling to see her.

But before he could answer, Jake was back, sliding behind the wheel.

'Sorry,' he said. 'Forgot to leave the AC on. I realized

you guys must be baking. Hot as balls today, isn't it?'

72 was still watching Lyra. But then he turned back toward the window.

'Yes,' he said. It was the first time he'd spoken directly to one of the humans except in anger, and Lyra noticed that Jake startled in his seat, as if he hadn't really expected a reply. 'Hot.'

TEN

LYRA HAD NEVER SEEN SO many houses or imagined that there could be so many people in the world. She knew the facts – she'd heard the nurses and doctors discussing them sometimes, problems with overpopulation, the division between rich and poor – and the nurses often watched TV or listened to the radio or watched videos on their phones when they were bored. But knowing something was different from seeing it: house upon house, many of them identical, so she felt dizzyingly as if she were going forward and also turning a circle; car after car lined up along the streets, grass trim and vividly green. And people everywhere. People driving or out on their lawns or waiting in groups on corners for reasons she couldn't fathom.

Jake stopped again at one of these houses, and Gemma got out of the car. Lyra watched through the window as a girl with black hair emerged from the house and bar-reled into Gemma's arms. Lyra was confused by this, as she was by Jake and Gemma's relationship, the casual way they spoke to each other, and the fact that Gemma was a replica but didn't know it. But she was confused by so much she didn't have the energy to worry about it.

For several minutes, Gemma and the other girl stood outside. Lyra tried to determine whether this second girl, the black-haired one, was a replica or a regular human but couldn't tell, although she was wearing human clothes and her hair was long. She used her hands a lot. Then the girl went inside, and Gemma returned to the car alone.

'April's going to open the gate,' she told Jake. She sounded breathless, though she hadn't walked far. 'You can park next to the pool house.'

Jake advanced the car and they corkscrewed left behind the house. Lyra saw a dazzling rectangle of water, still as a bath, which she knew must be a pool. Even though she couldn't swim, she had the urge to go under, to wash away what felt like days of accumulated dirt and mud and sweat. There were bathtubs in Postnatal, and even though they were too small to lie down in, Lyra had sometimes filled a tub and stepped in to her ankles after it was her turn to *tickle, engage, and maintain physical contact* with the new replicas.

When the gate closed behind them with a loud clang,

Lyra truly felt safe for the first time since leaving Haven. Contained. Controlled. Protected.

Next to the pool was a miniature version of the big house. Sliding doors opened into a large carpeted room that was dark and deliciously cold. The house was mostly white, which Lyra liked. It was like being back in Haven. Goose bumps ran along Lyra's arm, as if someone had just touched her. Where the carpet ran out was a kitchen alcove that Lyra identified only by its stove: it looked nothing like the kitchen in Stew Pot, a vast and shiny space filled with the hiss of steam from industrial dishwashers. Through an open door she saw a large bed, also made up with a white sheet and blankets and so many pillows she couldn't imagine what they were all for. And lined up on bookshelves next to the sofa: books. Dozens of books, four times as many as she'd seen in the nurses' break room, so many that in her excitement the titles blended together and she couldn't make out a single one.

She wanted to touch them. Their spines looked like different-colored candies the nurses exchanged sometimes, like the sugared lozenges the replicas got sometimes when they had coughs. But she was almost afraid to, afraid that if she did they would all blow apart. She wondered how long it would take her to read every book on the shelves. Months. Years, even. Maybe they would be allowed to stay here, in this clean and pretty room, with the sun that patterned the carpet and the soft hum of hidden air-conditioning.

At W-A-L-M-A-R-T, Gemma had bought Lyra and 72 new clothes – 'nothing fancy, and I had to guess how they would fit' – soap, shampoo, toothbrushes and tooth-paste, and more food, including cereal and milk, granola bars, cans of soup she said she could show them how to heat in the microwave, and at least a dozen frozen meals. She showed them where the shower was – a single shower stall, the first Lyra had ever seen – and apologized that there was only one bed.

'So, you know, you'll have to share, unless one of you wants to take the sofa,' she said. Lyra felt suddenly uncom-fortable, remembering Pepper and her unborn baby, and how she'd been found with her wrists open; the Christ-mas parties when the doctors got drunk and sometimes visited the dorms late at night, staggering on their feet and smelling sharply of alcohol swabs. That was why it was better for males and females to stay apart. 'I know you must be exhausted, so we're going to leave you alone for a bit, okay? Just don't go anywhere.'

Lyra didn't bother pointing out that they had nowhere to go.

'Get some sleep,' Gemma said. The more Lyra looked at her, the less she resembled Cassiopeia and her other genotypes. That was the funny thing about genotypes, something the nurses and doctors, who could never tell them apart, had never understood. If you looked, you could see differences in the way they moved and spoke and used their hands. Over time, their person-alities changed even the way that they looked. And of course Gemma was much heavier than Cassiopeia, and had long hair to her shoulders that looked soft to the touch. Gemma was nicer than Cassiopeia. More prone to worry, too. But they had the same stubbornness – that Lyra could see, too.

As soon as they were alone, Lyra went to the book-shelves. She could feel 72 watching her, but she didn't care and couldn't resist any longer. She reached up and ran a finger along the spines, each of them textured dif-ferently, some of them gloss-smooth and hard and others soft and crumbly like dirt. L-I-T-T-L-E W-O-M-E-N. *Little Women.* T-H-E G-O-L-D C-O-A-S-T. When she thought of *The Little Prince,* lost somewhere on the marshes, she still felt like crying. But these books made up for it, at least a little.

'You were telling the truth,' 72 said. He was watching her closely. 'You can read.' He made it sound like a bad thing.

'I told you. Dr. O'Donnell taught me.' She kept skip-ping her fingers over the titles and, as she did, read out loud: '*The Old Man and the Sea. The Long Walk. The Hunger Games.*'

He came to stand next to her. Again she could smell him, an earthy sweetness that made her feel slightly dizzy. She'd never found out which of the males Pepper had been with, although Cassiopeia had said a male doctor, because of what happened at the Christmas party, because Pepper had been chosen. But she wondered, now, whether instead it was 72.

'Is it hard?' he asked.

'At the beginning,' she said. She didn't know why she was thinking of Pepper. She took a step away from 72. 'Not so much when you get the hang of it.'

'I thought only people could read,' he blurted out. When she turned to look at him, surprised by the tone of his voice, he turned away. 'I'm going to get clean.'

A moment later, she heard the shower pipes shudder and the water start in the bathroom – a familiar sound that lulled her once again into exhaustion. She didn't understand 72 and his rapid changes of mood. But he'd chosen to stay with her. He hadn't left her behind. Maybe this complexity was a feature of the male replicas – she didn't know, had never been allowed to interact with them.

She removed the file she'd taken from its filthy pillowcase and placed it carefully on the desk below the windows. Although she had a roomful of books now – *a room full of books*, an idea so exciting it made goose bumps on her arms again – the folder, and the single sheet of paper it contained, was her final tether to home. She recognized an old patient report – she'd seen enough of her own reports to recognize a version of the form still in use. But she was too tired to read, and she left the folder open on the desk and returned to the shelves, no longer trying to make sense of the words, just admiring the way the letters looked, the angles and curls and scrolled loops of them.

'I'm all done now.'

She hadn't heard the shower go off or 72 emerge from the bathroom. She turned and froze. His skin, which had been streaked with blood and caked in a layer of sediment and crusted mud, was now as shiny and polished as a beach stone, and the color of new wood. His eyelashes, grayed by the ash, were long and black. A towel was wrapped around his waist. She was struck again by the strangeness of the male's body, the broadness of his shoulders and the torqued narrowness of his muscled waist.

'Thank you,' she said, snatching up the clothes Gemma had left for her. She was careful not to pass too close to him when she moved into the bathroom. She shut the door firmly, a little confused by the mechanism of the lock. At Haven, all the doors locked with keypads or codes, except for the bathrooms, which had no locks at all.

She stripped down and balled her filthy clothes in a corner. She had never showered alone before and it felt wonderful: the big echoey bathroom, the space, the aloneness of it. Was this how all people lived? It felt luxurious to her. She spent a few minutes adjusting the taps, delighted by how quickly the water responded. In Haven, there was never enough hot water. The soap Gemma had bought was lilac-scented and pale purple, and Lyra found herself thinking of 72, naked, washing with purple soap, and the urge to giggle bubbled up in her chest, followed by a wave of dizziness. She had to sit with her head between her legs and the water driving down on her shoulders until it passed.

She lathered and rinsed her scalp, scrubbed her ears with a pinkie finger, washed the soles of her feet so that they became so slippery it was treacherous to stand. Finally she felt clean. Even the towels here were better than they were at Haven, where they were thin and stiff from hundreds of washings. Her new clothes felt soft and clean. Gemma had bought her cotton underwear in different colors. She'd never had underwear that was anything but a bleached, dingy beige. Looking at herself in the mirror, she almost could have passed for a real person, except for the length of her hair. She fingered the scar above her right eyebrow. She had scars all over her body now, from spinal taps and harvesting operations to test her blood marrow, but when she was dressed, most of them were concealed. Not this one, though.

In the bedroom, she found 72 stretched out on top of the covers, staring up at the ceiling fan. He was wearing new jeans that Gemma had bought for him, and this fact seemed only to emphasize his shirtlessness and the smooth muscled lines of his chest and shoulders. She'd never noticed how beautiful bodies could be. She'd thought of them only as parts, machine components that serviced a whole. She'd been interested in the males, of course – curious about them – but she'd also learned that curiosity led to disappointment, that it was better not to want, not to look, not to wonder. But she was suddenly terrified of lying next to him, although she couldn't have said exactly why. Maybe because of what had happened to Pepper. But she thought it was more than that.

'What?' 72 sat up on his elbows. 'Why are you looking at me like that?'

'There's no reason.' Realizing she'd been staring, she forced herself to move to the bed. She slipped under the sheets – these, too, softer than any she'd ever known – and curled up with her knees to her chest, as far from 72 as possible. But still her heart was beating fast. She felt, or imagined she felt, warmth radiating off him. He smelled now a different kind of sweet, like shampoo and soap and fresh-scrubbed skin. For a long time they lay there together and she couldn't stop seeing him next to her, couldn't stop seeing his lashes lying on his cheeks when he closed his eyes and the high planes of his cheekbones and the darkness of his eyes.

He shifted in the bed. He put a hand on her waist. His hand was hot, burning hot.

'Lyra?' he whispered. His breath felt very close to her ear. She was terrified to move, terrified to turn and see how close he was.

'What?' she whispered back.

'I like your name,' he said. 'I wanted to say your name.'

Then the bed shifted again, and she knew he'd rolled over to go to sleep. Finally, after a long time, the tension in her body relaxed, and she slept, too.

When she woke up, it was dark, and for a confused second she thought she was back at Haven. She could smell dinner cooking in the Stew Pot and hear the nurses move between the cots, talking to one another. Then she opened her eyes and remembered. Someone had shut the bedroom door, but a wedge of light showed from the living room. Jake and Gemma were talking in low voices, and something was cooking. The smell brought sudden tears to Lyra's eyes. She was starving, hungrier than she'd been in weeks.

She eased out of bed, careful not to wake 72. She was vaguely disappointed to see they'd been sleeping with several feet of space between them. In her dream they had been entangled again, sweating and shivering in each other's arms. In her dream he'd said her name again, but into her mouth, whispering it.

In the big room, Jake was bent over a computer laptop that sat next to a soda on the coffee table. He smiled briefly at Lyra. She was startled – it had been a long time since anyone had smiled at her, probably since Dr. O'Donnell – and she tried to smile back, but her cheeks felt sore and wouldn't work properly. It didn't matter. She was too late. He'd already turned his attention back to the computer.

Immediately, Gemma was moving away from the stove with a bowl, skirting the table that divided the kitchen from the library   Lyra thought it must be called a library, anyway, since Dr. O'Donnell had told her that libraries were places you could read books for free. 'Here,' Gemma said. 'Chili. From a can. Sorry,' she added, when Lyra stared, 'I can't cook.'

But Lyra had only been wondering at all her freedoms, at the fact that Gemma knew how to shop and get food and clothing. Wherever she'd been made, she must have lived for most of her life among real people.

'You need to eat,' Gemma said firmly, and seemed

surprised – and pleased – when Lyra took the bowl and spoon and began to eat so quickly she burned the roof of her mouth. She didn't even bother sitting down, both thrilled and disturbed by the fact that there was no one to yell at her or tell her to keep her seat.

'Transmissible spongiform encephalopathies,' Jake said out loud, still bending over his computer. 'That's a category of disease. Mad cow is a TSE.'

'Okay.' Gemma drew out the last syllable. 'But what does that mean?' She went to sit next to Jake on the couch, and Lyra licked the bowl clean, after making sure neither of them was looking. Jake kept turning his soda can, adjusting it so that the small square napkin beneath it was parallel to the table's edge.

'I don't know.' Jake scrubbed his forehead with a hand and fixed his laptop so this, too, was parallel. 'There are just references to it in the report.'

Lyra saw that next to Jake's computer was the file she'd stolen from Haven. She set her bowl down on the table with a clatter. 'You – you shouldn't be looking at that,' she said.

'Why not?' Jake raised an eyebrow. 'You stole it, didn't you?'

'Yes,' Lyra said evenly. 'But that's different.'

'It's not like they'll miss it now. The whole place is an ash heap.'

In Lyra's head, she saw all of Haven reduced to a column of smoke. Sometimes the bodies that burned came back to Haven in the form of smoke, in a sweet smell that tickled the back of the throat. The nurses hated it, but Lyra didn't.

'Jake,' Gemma said.

He shrugged. 'Sorry. But it's true.'

He was right, obviously. She couldn't possibly get in trouble now for stealing the file or allowing someone else to see it – at least, no more trouble than she was already in. Jake went back to thumping away at the computer. Gemma reached out and drew the file onto her lap. Lyra watched her puzzle over it, frowning. Maybe Gemma couldn't read?

But after a minute, Gemma said, 'Lyra, do you know what this means? It says the patient – the replica, I mean' – she looked up as though for approval, and Lyra nodded – 'was in the yellow cluster.'

The yellow cluster. The saddest cluster of all. Lyra remembered all those tiny corpses with their miniature yellow bracelets, all of them laid out for garbage collection. The nurses had come through wearing gloves and masks that made them look like insects, double wrapping the bodies, disposing of them.

'The Yellows died,' she said, and Gemma flinched. 'There were about a hundred of them, all from the younger crops. Crops,' she went on, when Gemma still looked confused, 'separate the different generations. But colors are for clusters. So I'm third crop, green cluster.' She held up her bracelet, where everything was printed neatly. *Gen-3, TG-GR*. Generation 3, Testing Group Green. She didn't understand why Gemma looked sick to her stomach. 'They must have made a mistake with the Yellows. Sometimes they did that. Made mistakes. The Pinks died, too.'

'They all died?' Jake asked.

Lyra nodded. 'They got sick.'

'Oh my God.' Gemma brought a hand to her mouth. She seemed sad, which Lyra didn't understand. Gemma didn't know anyone in the yellow cluster. And they were just replicas. 'It says here she was only fourteen months.'

Lyra almost pointed out that the youngest had died when she was only three or four months, but didn't.

'You said colors are for clusters,' Jake said slowly. 'But clusters of what?'

Lyra shrugged. 'There are different clusters, and we all get different variants.'

'Variants of what?' he pressed.

Lyra didn't know, exactly, but she wasn't going to admit it. 'Medicine,' she said firmly, hoping he wouldn't ask her anything more.

Gemma sucked in a deep breath. 'Look, Jake. It's

signed by Dr. Saperstein, just like you said.'

'Dr. Saperstein is in charge of the growth of new crops of replicas,' Lyra said. Despite the fact that she was still annoyed at Jake and Gemma for looking at the file – the *private* file, *her* file – she moved closer to the couch, curious to know what they were doing. 'He signs all the death certificates.' Beneath his was a second signature, a name she knew well. Nurse Em had been one of the nicer ones: Nurse Em had taken care when inserting the needles, to make sure it wouldn't hurt; she had sometimes told jokes. 'Nurse Em signed, too.'

'Nurse Em.' Gemma closed her eyes and leaned back.

'Holy shit,' Jake said, and Gemma opened her eyes again, giving Jake a look Lyra couldn't decipher.

'Nurse Em was one of the nicest ones. But she left,' Lyra said. An old memory surfaced. She was alone in a hallway, watching Dr. O'Donnell and Nurse Em through a narrow crack in a door. Dr. O'Donnell had her hands on Nurse Em's shoulders and Nurse Em was crying. 'Think of what's right, Emily,' Dr. O'Donnell said. 'You're a good person. You were just in over your head.' But then Nurse Em had wrenched away from her, knocking over a mop, and Lyra had backed quickly away from the door before Nurse Em barreled through it.

But that couldn't have been a real memory – she remembered a janitor's closet but that couldn't be right, not when the nurses and doctors had break rooms. And Nurse Em had been crying – but why would Dr. O'Donnell have made Nurse Em cry?

'Let me see that.' Jake took the file from Gemma and leaned over the computer again. Lyra liked watching the impression of his fingers on the keys, the way a stream of letters appeared as though by magic on the screen, far too fast for her to read. *Click. Click. Click.* The screen was now full of tiny type, photographs, diagrams. It was dizzying. She couldn't even tell one letter from another. 'This report – all of this terminology, TSEs and neural decay and protein folding – it's all about prions.'

'Prions?' Gemma said. She'd clearly never heard the word before, and Lyra was glad that for once she wasn't the one who was confused.

'Bacteria, viruses, fungi, and prions,' Jake said, squinting at the screen. 'Prions are infectious particles. They're proteins, basically, except they're folded all wrong.'

'Replicas are full of prions,' Lyra said, proud of herself for knowing this. The doctors had never said so directly, but she had paid attention: at Haven, there was very little to do but listen. That was the purpose of the spinal taps and all the harvesting – to remove tissue samples to test for prion penetration. Often when replicas died they were dissected, their bones drilled open, for the same reason. She knew that prions were incredibly important – Dr.

Saperstein was always talking about engineering prions to be better and faster-acting – but she didn't know what they were, exactly.

Jake gave her a funny look, as if he had swallowed a bad-tasting medicine.

'I still don't get it,' Gemma said. 'What do prions do?'

He read out loud: '"Prion infectivity is present at high levels in brain or other central nervous system tissues, and at slightly lower levels in the spleen, lymph nodes, bone marrow. . . ." Wait. That's not it. "If a prion enters a healthy organism, it induces existing, properly folded proteins to convert into the disease-associated, misfolded prion form. In that sense, they are like cloning devices."' He looked up at Gemma, and then looked quickly down again. '"The prion acts as a template to guide the misfolding of more proteins into prion form, leading to an exponential increase of prions in the central nervous system and subsequent symptoms of prion disease. This can take months or even years."' He put a hand through his hair again and Lyra watched it fall, wondering whether 72's hair would grow out now, whether it would fall just the same way. '"Prion disease is spread when a person or animal ingests infected tissue, as in the case of bovine SE, or mad cow disease. Prions may also contaminate the water supply, given the presence of blood or other secretions. . . ."'

'So prions are a kind of disease?' Gemma asked.

'The bad kind of prions are disease,' Jake said quietly.

'That can't be right,' Lyra said. She was having trouble following everything that Jake was saying, but she knew that there, at least, he was wrong. She knew that replicas were physically inferior to normal humans – the cloning process was still imperfect, and they were vulnerable. That was the word the doctors and nurses always used when they lined up vitamins and pills, sometimes a dozen in a row. But she'd always thought – and she didn't know why she'd thought this, but she knew it had to do with things overheard, sensed, and implied – that prions were *good*. She'd always had the impression that this was a single way in which replicas were superior to humans: their tissue was humming with prions that could be extracted from them.

She felt a curious tickle at the back of her throat, almost as if she had to sneeze. Sweat prickled in her armpits.

Jake wouldn't look at her. She was used to that.

'Listen to this.' Jake had pulled up new writing – so many lines of text Lyra felt vaguely suffocated. How many words could there possibly be? 'Google Saperstein and prions and an article comes up from back in the early 1990s. Saperstein was speaking at a conference about biological terrorism. "Chemical weapons and viral and bacterial agents are problematic. Our soldiers risk exposure even as the weapons are deployed against our enemies. War is changing. Our enemies are changing, growing radicalized and more diverse. I believe the future of biological warfare lies in the isolation of a faster-acting prion that can be distributed via food supply chains.'" Jake was sweating. And Lyra had been sweating too, but now she was cold all over. It felt like she had to use the bathroom, but she couldn't move. "'We might cripple terrorist groups by disseminating doctored medications and vaccinations, which will be unknowingly spread by health care workers in dangerous and remote environments immune to normal modes of attack.

"'All known prion diseases in mammals affect the structure of the brain or other neural tissue and all are currently untreatable and universally fatal. Imagine'" – Jake was barely whispering – "'terrorist cells or enemy insurgents unable to think, walk, or speak. Paralyzed or exterminated.'"

'Oh my God,' Gemma said. She brought a hand to her lips. 'That's awful.'

From nowhere a vision came to Lyra of a vast, dust-filled field, and thousands of bodies wrapped in dark paper like the Yellows had been, still and silent under a pale-blue sky.

What was it that Jake had read?

All known prion diseases in mammals . . . are currently

untreatable and universally fatal.

'Jesus.' Jake leaned back and closed his eyes. For a long time, no one said anything. Lyra felt strangely as if she had left her body behind, as if she no longer existed at all. She was a wall. She was the floor and the ceiling. 'That's the answer to what they were doing at Haven.' Although he'd addressed Gemma, when he opened his eyes again, he looked directly at Lyra, and immediately she slammed back into her body and hated him for it. 'Prions live in human tissue. Don't you see?'

Lyra could see. But she couldn't say so. Her voice had dried up. She was filled with misfolded crystals, like tiny slivers of glass, slowly cutting her open from the inside. It was Gemma who spoke.

'They've been experimenting on the replicas,' she said slowly. She wouldn't look at Lyra. 'They've been observing the effects of the disease.'

'Not just experimenting on them,' Jake said, and his voice broke. 'Incubating them. Gemma, they've been using the replicas to *make* prions. They've been growing the disease *inside* them.'

ELEVEN

'I TOLD YOU.'

Lyra turned and saw 72, his cheek still crisscrossed with lines from the pillow. He was looking not at Jake or Gemma but directly at Lyra, and she couldn't read his expression. She had spent her whole life listening to doctors talk about the workings of the lungs and liver, the blood-brain barrier, and white blood cell counts, but she had never heard a single one explain how faces worked, what they meant, how to read them.

'I told you,' he said again, softer this time, 'they never cared. They were never trying to protect us. It was a lie.'

'You knew?' she said.

He stared at her. 'Didn't you?' His voice was quiet. 'Didn't you, really?'

She looked away, ashamed. He was right, of course. Everything had fallen away, the final veil, the game she'd been playing for years, the lies she'd been telling herself. It all made sense now. Numbers instead of names, *it* instead of *she* or *he*. *Are you going to teach the rats to play chess?* They were disposable and always had been. It wasn't that they were more prone to diseases, to failures of the liver and lungs. They'd been manufactured to die.

All the times she felt nauseous or dizzy or couldn't remember where she was or where she was going: not side effects of the treatment, but of the disease. Actually, not side effects at all.

Symptoms.

Gemma stood up. 'We've done enough for the night,' she said to Jake. Lyra knew that Gemma must feel sorry for them. Or maybe she was only scared. Maybe she thought the disease was contagious.

She wondered how long she had. Six months? A year? It seemed so stupid to have run. What was the point, since she was just going to die anyway? Maybe she should have let the guards shoot her after all.

Jake closed his computer. 'It's after ten o'clock,' he said, rubbing his eyes. 'My aunt's coming back from Decatur tomorrow. I've got to go home.'

'Let's pick up in the morning, okay? We'll figure out what to do in the morning.' Gemma addressed the words to Jake, but Lyra had a feeling she meant the words for her.

'Are you going to be okay?' Jake asked. He lifted a hand as if he was going to touch Lyra's shoulder, but she took a quick step backward and he let his hand fall.

Lyra shrugged. It hardly mattered. She kept thinking about what Jake had said. *They've been growing the disease inside them.* Like the glass hothouses where Haven grew vegetables and fruit. She pictured her body blown full of air and proteins misfolded into snowflake shapes. She pictured the illustration she'd once seen of a pregnant woman and the child curled inside her womb. They had implanted her. She was carrying an alien child, something deadly and untreatable.

'If you need anything, just give a shout,' Gemma said.

'Here.' Jake bent over and scrawled something on a piece of paper. Normally Lyra loved to see a person writing by hand, the way the letters simply fell from the pen, but now she didn't care. There was no help Jake could give her. No help anyone could give her. 'This is my telephone number. Have you used a telephone before?'

'I know what a telephone is,' Lyra said. Though she had never used one herself, the nurses hardly did anything but, and as a little kid she'd sometimes picked up random things – tubes of toothpaste, bars of soap, prescription bottles – and pretended to speak into them, pretended there was someone in another world who would answer.

Jake nodded. 'This is my address. Here. Just in case. Can you read this?'

Lyra nodded but couldn't bring herself to meet Jake's eyes.

For several minutes after Gemma and Jake left, Lyra stayed where she was, sitting on the couch. 72 moved around the room silently, picking things up and then putting them down. She was unaccountably angry at him. He had predicted this. That meant it was his fault.

'When did you know?' she asked. '*How* did you know?'

He glanced at her, and then turned his attention back to a small bubble of glass: plastic snow swirled down when he inverted it. 'I told you. I didn't know *exactly*,' he said. 'But I knew they were making us sick. I knew that was the point.' He said it casually.

'How?' Lyra repeated.

He set the snow globe down, and Lyra watched a flurry of artificial snow swirl down on the two tiny figures contained forever in their tiny bubble world: a stretch of plastic beach, a single palm tree. She felt sorry for them. She understood them.

'I didn't ever not know,' he said, frowning. To her surprise, he came to sit next to her on the couch. He still smelled good. This made her ache, for some reason. As if inside of her, someone was driving home a nail. 'I was sick once, as a little kid. Very sick. I remember they thought I was going to die. I went to the Funeral Home.' He looked down at his hands. 'They were excited. When they thought I couldn't understand them anymore, they were excited.'

Lyra said nothing. She thought of lying on the table after seeing Mr. I, the happy chatter of the researchers above her, their sandwich-smelling breath and the way they laughed when her eyes refused to follow their penlight.

'When I was a kid I used to pretend,' he said. 'I would pretend I was an ant or a lizard or a bird. Anything else. I would catch roaches sometimes coming out of the drains. All the nurses hated the roaches. But even they were better off than we were. They could get out.' He opened his palm, staring as if he didn't recognize it, then closed it again in a fist. 'It would be better,' he said, slightly louder, 'if they'd hated us. But they didn't.'

About this, too, he was right. Worse than Nurse-Don't-Even-Think-About-It, worse than the ones who were afraid, were the ones who hardly noticed. Who would look not at the replicas but through them, who could talk about what to eat for dinner even as they bundled up dead bodies for burning.

'Why didn't you tell me?' Lyra asked.

'I tried,' he said. 'Besides, what good would it do?'

She shook her head. She needed someone to blame.

She had never been so angry before – she hadn't even thought she had the right. People, real people, believed they deserved things and were angry when they didn't get them. Replicas deserved nothing, received nothing, and so were never angry.

What kind of God was it, she wondered, who made people who would do what they had done to her?

'Is that why you ran away?' Lyra asked. She felt like crying. She wasn't in physical pain and yet she felt as if something had changed in her body, as if someone had put tubes in her chest and everything was entangled.

'No,' 72 said. 'Not exactly.'

'Why, then?'

He just shook his head. She doubted whether he knew himself. Maybe only for a change. Then he said, 'We can't stay here, you know.'

Lyra hadn't expected this. 'Why not?'

'We're not safe here,' he said, and his expression turned again, folded up. 'I told you. I don't trust them. They aren't replicas.'

'The girl is,' Lyra said.

He frowned. 'She doesn't know it,' he said. 'No one's told her.'

'But we don't have anywhere else to go,' she said, and once again realized how true it was. How big was the world? She had no idea. They'd driven for what felt like hours today, and there had been no end to the roads and shopping complexes, streets and houses. And yet Gemma had told her they were still in Florida. How much farther did it all go on? 'Besides, what does it matter?' *We'll just die anyway,* she almost added, but she knew he understood.

'I didn't come this far to be a toy,' he said. 'I could have gone back to Haven for that.'

Lyra didn't know what he meant, exactly, but she could guess from his tone of voice. 'They've been good to us,' she said. 'They helped us. They fed us. They gave us clothes and somewhere to sleep.'

'Exactly. So what do they want? They must want something. They're people,' he said. 'That's what they do. Don't you see? That's all they *ever* do. They want.'

Was that true? She didn't know. What had Dr. O'Donnell wanted from her? Or Nurse Em, who always smiled at the replicas, who had once told Lyra she had pretty eyes, who saved up her old ferry tokens to give to the young kids to play checkers with?

But maybe that was why they had left Haven: they did not fit in. She still didn't understand what made people so different from replicas, had never been able to understand it. And she had wanted things too, in her life. She had wanted to learn to read. She had been hungry, cold, and tired, and wanted food and her bed. But it was true she had never hurt anyone to get what she wanted.

Was that what made her less than human?

'Is that enough for you?' 72 said. He scared her when he looked this way, and reminded her of the statue in the courtyard at Haven, whose face, deformed by rain, was sightless and cold. 'Someone to feed you and order you around, tell you when to sleep? Like a dog?'

She stood. 'Well, what's the difference?' she said, and she could tell she'd surprised him, because he flinched. She was surprised, too. Her voice was much louder than she'd expected. 'We're replicas, aren't we? We might as well be dogs. That's how they think of us anyway. That's what we were made for. To be dogs – or rats. You weren't pretending all those years ago. You *were* a roach.'

He stared at her for a long second. She could see his chest rising with his breath and knew that beneath his skin hundreds of tiny muscles were contracting in his face even to hold it there, still, watching her. The idea of him and what he was made of, all the different fragile parts spun together, made her dizzy.

Finally he looked away. 'That's why I ran,' he said. 'I wanted to know whether we could be good for anything else. I wanted to try.' To her surprise, he smiled, just a little. 'Besides, even roaches run away. Rats, too.'

They went through the guesthouse, looking for anything that would be useful. In a bedroom closet beneath extra pillows they found an old backpack, which they filled with the remaining granola bars and bottles of water, plus the bathroom things that Gemma had bought for them. Lyra knew they likely wouldn't need soap but couldn't stand to leave the pretty, paper-wrapped bars behind, so different from anything she'd ever owned.

Jake had left his cell phone charging in the corner and 72 took it, although they had no one to call. It excited Lyra to have it in their possession, to touch the screen and leave fingerprints there. Only people had cell phones.

They took knives from the kitchen, a blanket from the otherwise empty cabinet by the bed. She didn't feel guilty about stealing from Jake and Gemma, who had helped them. She felt nothing at all. Maybe, she thought, the nurses had been right about replicas. Maybe they didn't have souls.

By then the main house had gone dark. 72 suggested they turn the light off too, so in case Jake and Gemma were looking out for them, they would believe Lyra and 72 had gone to bed. They waited there, in the dark, for another twenty minutes just to be sure. They sat again on the sofa side by side, and Lyra thought of her dream of entanglement, all those inches and inches of exposed skin. She was glad he couldn't see her.

Finally he touched her elbow. 'It's time,' he said. His face in the dark was different colors of shadow.

Outside, the sound of insects and tree frogs startled Lyra: a rhythmic and almost mechanical thrumming that recalled the throaty roar of Mr. I.

'Wait.' 72 nudged her. Gemma was curled up on a plastic deck chair, still wearing her clothes, using several colorful towels as blankets. Lyra was confused. Had she been watching them? Trying to make sure they didn't escape? She couldn't imagine why she would have otherwise chosen to sleep outside.

Before she could stop him, 72 was already moving closer, stepping very carefully. Lyra followed him with a growing sense of unease. Gemma's face in the moonlight looked so much like Cassiopeia's, she wanted to reach out and lay a hand on Gemma's chest, to feel her breathing and believe Cassiopeia had come back to life. But she didn't, obviously.

Lying next to Gemma on the pool deck was an open notebook. A pen had rolled into the binding. As always Lyra was drawn to the words scribbled across the page. They appeared to glow faintly in the moonlight. Gemma's writing, she thought, was very beautiful. The words reminded her of bird tracks, of birds themselves, pecking their way proudly across the page.

Then a familiar name caught her attention: Emily Huang. Nurse Em.

She placed a finger on the page, mouthing the words

written directly beneath the name. Palm Grove. The words meant nothing to her. There were other names on the page, all of them unfamiliar except for Dr. Saperstein's, which was joined by a small notation to the Home Foundation. She didn't know what that was, either, but beneath it was at last another word she recognized: Gainesville. This, she knew, was a place. A big place. Jake and Gemma had argued about whether they should be getting off at the highway exit to Gainesville and Jake had said, *No one wants to go to Gainesville,* and then Gemma had said, *Except the half a million people who live there.* She figured that Palm Grove might be a place, too.

She took the notebook. Jake had taken the file folder she'd stolen, so it was a fair trade. She straightened up and saw that 72 was rifling through Gemma's bag to get to her wallet. She grabbed his shoulder, shaking her head. Once, years ago, Don't-Even-Think-About-It's wallet had been stolen from the mess hall, and she remembered how terrible it was, how all the replicas' beds were searched and their cubbies turned out, how Don't-Even-Think-About-It was in a foul mood for days and backhanded Lyra for looking at her wrong. They had found it, finally, in a hole torn out of the underside of Ursa Major's mattress, along with all the other things she'd scavenged over the years: dirty socks and a lost earring, ferry tokens, soda can tabs, gum wrappers.

But she couldn't speak without risking waking Gemma, and even as she watched he removed a wedge of money from her wallet and, pocketing it, returned the wallet to her purse. Lyra put back the notebook anyway. She wasn't likely to forget Palm Grove.

They scaled the gate because they didn't know how to make it work and, once they were on the other side, on a street made liquid dark and shiny by the streetlights, began to walk. Bound on either side by houses with their hedges and gates, Lyra did not feel so afraid. But soon they reached a road that stretched blackly into the empty countryside, and she felt a kind of terror she associated with falling: so much space, more space than she'd ever imagined.

Only then did Lyra speak. They'd gone too far to be heard by anyone. Besides, she hated the emptiness of the road and the streetlamps bent silently over their work, like tall arms planted in the earth.

'I know someone who can help us,' she said. Their feet crunched on the gravel at the side of the road. Now she was grateful for the tree frogs. At least they were company.

'Help us?' 72 tilted his head back to look at the sky and the stars spread above them. She couldn't tell whether he was frightened, but she doubted it. He didn't seem afraid of anything. Even dying. Maybe he'd just had time to get used to it. She had known that replicas were frailer than real people, more prone to illness, sicklier and smaller. But on some level she'd believed that at Haven, she might be safe.

'I want to know more,' she said. 'I want to know why they did this to us. Why they made us sick. I want to know if there's a cure.'

He stopped walking. He stared at her. 'There's no cure,' he said.

'Not that we know of,' she said. 'But you said yourself you didn't know exactly what they were doing at Haven. There could be a cure. They could have developed one.'

'Why would they?' he said. He looked as if he was trying not to smile. In that moment, she hated him. She'd never met someone who could make her have so many different feelings – who could make her feel at all, really.

'I don't know,' she said. 'I don't know why they did anything.'

He looked at her, chewing on the inside of his cheek. She supposed that he wasn't ugly after all. She supposed that he was beautiful, in his own way, strange and angular, like the spiky plants that grew between the walkways at Haven, with a fan of dark-green leaves. She'd overheard Gemma say that, on the phone in the car earlier. Maybe she hadn't thought Lyra was listening. *There's a girl and a boy,* she'd said. *The girl is sick or something. The boy is* . . . And she'd lowered her voice to a whisper. *Beautiful*. Lyra had never really thought of faces as beautiful before, although she had enjoyed the geometry of Jake's face, and she supposed, in retrospect, that Dr. O'Donnell had been beautiful. At least she was in Lyra's memory.

She wondered if she herself was ugly.

Two lights appeared in the distance. She raised a hand to her eyes, momentarily dazzled and afraid, and then realized it was only an approaching car. But it began to slow and she was afraid again. Somehow, instinctively, she and 72 took hands. His were large and dry and much nicer than the hands of the doctors, which, wrapped in disposable gloves, always felt both clammy and cold, like something dead.

'You kids all right?' The man in the car had to lean all the way across the seat to talk to them through the open window.

72 nodded. Lyra was glad. She couldn't speak.

'Funny place for a stroll,' he said. 'You be careful, okay? There's cars come down this road eighty, ninety miles an hour.'

He started to roll up his window and Lyra exhaled, relieved and also stunned. If he'd recognized them as replicas, it didn't seem like it. Maybe the differences weren't as obvious as she thought.

'Hello,' she blurted out, and the window froze and

then buzzed down again. 'Hello,' she repeated, taking a step toward the car and ignoring 72, who hissed something, a warning, probably. 'Have you heard of Palm Grove?'

'Palm Grove, Florida?' The man had thick, fleshy fingers, and a cigarette burned between them. 'You weren't thinking of walking there, were you?' He said it half laughing, as if he'd made a joke. But when she didn't smile, he squinted at her through the smoke unfurling from his cigarette. 'The twelve goes straight up the coast to Palm Grove on its way to Tallahassee. If that's where you're headed, you can't miss the bus depot. But it's a hike. Five or six miles at least.'

Lyra nodded, even though she didn't know what he meant by *the twelve*, or how far five or six miles was.

'Won't catch a bus this late, though,' the man said. 'Hope you got a place to stay the night.' He was still staring at her, but now his eyes ticked over her shoulder to 72 and back again. Something shifted in his face. 'Hey. You sure you're okay? You don't look too good.'

Lyra backed quickly away from the car. 'I'm fine,' she said. 'We're fine.'

He stared at them for another long moment. 'Watch out for the drivers down this stretch, like I said. They'll be halfway to Miami before they realize they got you.'

Then he was gone and his taillights became the red tips

of two cigarettes and then vanished.

'You shouldn't speak to them,' 72 said. 'You shouldn't speak to any of them.'

'He spoke to me,' Lyra said. 'Besides, what harm did it do?'

72 just shook his head, still staring in the direction the car had gone, as if he expected it might rematerialize. 'What's in Palm Grove?'

'Someone who might be able to help,' Lyra said carefully.

'Who?' 72 was backlit by the streetlamp and all in shadow.

She knew he might refuse to go with her, and if he did, she would still find her way to Palm Grove. They owed each other nothing. It was chance that had kept them together so far. Still, the idea of being completely on her own was terrifying. She had never been alone at Haven. At the very least the guards had always been watching.

But she saw no way to lie convincingly. She knew no one, had no one, in the outside world, and he knew that. 'She was a nurse at Haven,' she said.

'No,' he said immediately, and began walking again, kicking at the gravel and sending it skipping away across the road.

'Wait.' She got a hand around his arm, the one crisscrossed with all those vivid white scars. She turned him around and had a sudden shock: just for a second her body did something, *told* her something, she didn't understand.

'No,' he said again.

She dropped his arm. She didn't know what she wanted from him but she did, and that made her feel confused and exhausted and unhappy. 'She's not like the other ones,' she said. Dr. O'Donnell had said, *You're a good person,* even as Nurse Em sobbed so that snot bubbled in her nostrils. *You want to make things right. I know you do.* That had to mean it was true.

'How do you know that?' 72 said. He took a step forward, and Lyra nearly tripped trying to get away from him. She didn't want to be anywhere near him, not after what had happened. Even standing several inches away she felt a current moving through her body, something warm and alive, something that whispered. She hated it.

'I just know,' she said. 'She left Haven. She wanted to help us.' In her head she added, *Because Dr. O'Donnell believed in her. Because Dr. O'Donnell was always right.* She wished, more than anything, that she knew where Dr. O'Donnell lived, and imagined once again the feel of Dr. O'Donnell's hand skimming the top of her head. *Mother.* She thought Dr. O'Donnell's house must be all white and very clean, just like Haven. But maybe instead of being on the ocean it was in a field, and the smell of flowers came through the open windows on the wind.

Another car went by, this time with a punch of music and rhythm. Then another car. This time the window went down and a boy had his head out of it, yelling something she couldn't make out. An empty can missed her head by only a few inches.

For a long time, 72 just stared at her. She wondered again whether she was ugly, whether he realized that now, the same way she knew now that he was beautiful. As a replica it had never mattered, and it shouldn't matter now, but it did. She wondered if this was the human world rubbing off on her, whether she might become more human by becoming uglier, by accepting it.

She didn't want to be ugly in his eyes.

Finally he said, 'We should get off the road and find somewhere to sleep for the night.' She thought he almost smiled. 'Well, we can't sleep here. And you heard him. There are no buses until morning.'

They moved off the road and walked instead through a scrum of crushed paper cups, cigarette butts, and empty plastic bags. Soon they came to an area of buildings groveling under the lights that encircled them, including a sign in neon that read *Liquorz*. Lit as they were in starkness and isolation, they reminded Lyra briefly and painfully of Haven at night when, sleepily, she would get up to use the bathroom and would look out and see the guard towers and floodlights making harsh angles out of the landscape.

One of the buildings' pitched roofs tapered into the form of a cross and so she thought it must be a church, although otherwise it was identical to its neighbors: shingle-sided and gray, separated by a narrow band of cracked pavement from a gas station and a diner, both closed for the night. Lyra saw that someone had written *I was here* across the plywood and wasn't surprised. In a world this big, it must be easy to get lost and need reminders.

Behind the church was a weed-choked field that extended toward another road in the distance, this one even busier. Headlights beaded down the thin fold in the dark like blood along a needle. But the noise was transformed by all the space into a constant shushing, like the sound of ocean waves. They shook out their blanket here, and Lyra was glad that they'd decided to sleep so close to the road and the lights. The space in between, the nothingness and distance, frightened her.

The blanket was small, and when they lay down side by side, on their backs, they couldn't help but touch. Lyra didn't know how she would sleep. Her body was telling her something again, urging her to move, to run, to touch him. Instead she crossed her arms tightly and stared at the sky until the stars sharpened in her vision. She tried to pick out Cassiopeia. When she was little, she'd liked to pretend that stars were really lights anchoring distant islands, as if she wasn't looking up but only out across a dark sea. She knew the truth now but still found stars comforting, especially in their sameness. A sky full of burning replicas.

'Do you know more stories?'

Lyra was startled. She'd thought 72 was asleep. His eyes were closed and one arm was thrown across his face, so his voice was muffled.

'What do you mean?'

He withdrew the arm but kept his eyes closed, so she was free to look at him. Again, his face looked very bare in the dark, as if during the day he wore a different face that only now, with his eyes closed, had rubbed away. She noticed the particular curve of his lips and nostrils, the smooth arrangement of his cheekbones, and wanted to touch and explore them with her fingers. 'You can read. You told that story on the marshes. About the girl, Matilda. You must know more, then.'

She thought of *The Little Prince* and its soft cover, creased through the illustration, its smudgy papers and its smell, now lost forever. She squeezed her ribs hard, half wishing she would crack. 'Only one more good one,' she said.

'Tell it,' he said.

Again she was surprised. 'What?'

This time he opened his eyes, turning slightly to face

her. 'Tell it,' he said. And then: 'Please.' His lashes were very long. His lips looked like fruit, something to suck on. Now he did smile. She saw his teeth flash white in the dark.

She looked away. The stars spun a little, dizzy above her. 'There,' she said, lifting an arm to point. 'See that star?'

'Which one?'

'That one. The little twinkly one, just next to the one that looks almost blue.'

It didn't matter whether he was looking at exactly the same star as she was. But after a moment he said, 'I see it.'

'That's Planet B-612,' she said. 'It's an asteroid, actually. And that's where the Little Prince comes from.' She closed her eyes, and in her head she heard echoes of Dr. O'Donnell's voice, smelled lemon soap, watched a finger tracking across the page, pointing out different words. 'It's a small planet, but it's his. There are three volcanoes on the surface, one active, two inactive. And there are baobab plants that try and overgrow everything. There's a rose, too. The Little Prince loves the rose.' This was the part of the book that had most confused her, but she said it anyway, because she knew it was important.

'But who *is* the Little Prince?' 72 asked.

'The Little Prince has golden hair, a scarf, and a lovable laugh,' Lyra said, reciting from memory.

'What's lovable?' 72 asked.

Lyra shifted. 'It means . . .' She didn't know. 'I guess it means someone loves you.'

72 didn't say anything. She was going to continue her story, but she felt a bad pressure in her chest, as if someone was feeding a tube into her lungs.

'How do you get to be loved?' 72 asked. His voice was quiet, slurred by sleep.

'I don't know,' Lyra answered honestly. She was glad when he fell asleep, or at least pretended to. She didn't feel like telling a story much after that.

TWELVE

IN THE MORNING THEY WERE woken by a shout. Lyra thought they must have been spotted. Instead she saw a man in thick gloves loading trash from the Dumpsters into an enormous truck. Momentarily hypnotized, she watched the trash flattened by machinery that looked like metal teeth. The smell was sweet and vaguely sickening. Still, she was hungry.

Then she remembered the money they'd stolen from Gemma's wallet. 72 was awake now too, and the man in the gloves stared at them as they stood and rolled up the blanket, stuffing it in their backpack, but said nothing. Lyra was beginning to understand that humans outside Haven didn't seem to care about them. Maybe their world was simply too big. They couldn't pay attention to all of it.

72 was hungry too, so they went to the diner next to the

gas station and took turns in the bathroom washing their faces and hands. Lyra even wet her scalp and brushed her teeth. There was a stack of small paper cups and electric-blue mouthwash in a dispenser above the sink. When she returned to the table, 72 was fumbling with Jake's stolen phone.

'It won't stop ringing,' he said. And in fact the phone lit up in his hands, sending out a tinny musical sound.

'Let me try,' she said. She'd seen cell phones before but had only ever handled one once, when Nurse Em, years ago, had shown Lyra pictures of her dog at home on the mainland. A Pomeranian. White and fluffy but otherwise ratlike, Lyra had thought, but hadn't said so. Maybe the dog was still alive. She didn't know how long dogs normally lived, and whether they outlasted replicas.

She managed to get the phone to stop ringing and returned it to 72, who put it in his pocket. She wondered why he liked carrying it around if they had no one to call. Maybe it was because of what he'd said and why he'd escaped: just to see what it was like. Just for a little.

The menu was so full of writing that Lyra's head hurt looking at it. There was a whole section named *Eggs*. How many different ways could eggs be eaten? At Haven they were always scrambled, crispy and brown on the bottom.

'It's a waste,' 72 said. He seemed angry about the

menu. 'All this food.' But she thought he was just angry about not being able to read. He made no mention of the story she'd started to tell him last night, of the Little Prince, and Lyra was glad. His question was still bothering her, as was the feeling she'd had afterward, a strange emptiness, as if she was already dead.

A woman came to ask them what they wanted to eat. Lyra had never been asked that question before, and in that moment she deeply missed the Haven mess hall and the food lit orange beneath heating lamps and the way it was deposited onto their plates by sour-faced women wearing hairnets. 72 ordered coffee and eggs. So she ordered the same thing. The eggs were burned on the bottom and tasted like they did at Haven, which made her feel better.

They paid with two of Gemma's bills and got a bewildering assortment of change back. Lyra couldn't help but think of the younger replicas and how they would have loved to play with all those coins, skipping them or rolling them across the floor, seeing who could get the most heads in a row. She wondered where all the other replicas were, and imagined them in a new Haven, this one perhaps on a mountain and surrounded by the clean smell of pine, before remembering what they were. Carriers.

Disposable.

Lyra asked the waitress about Palm Grove, and she directed them up the road to the bus depot. 'Can't miss it,' she said. 'Just take the twelve up toward Tallahassee. Soon as you see the water park, that's Palm Grove. You kids heading to the water park?' Lyra shook her head. The woman popped her gum. 'That's too bad. They got one slide three stories tall. Cobra, it's called. And today's gonna be a bruiser. Where you kids from?'

But Lyra only shook her head again, and they stepped out into the heat.

By the time they reached the bus depot, Lyra's shoes felt as if they were rubbing all the skin off her feet. She wasn't used to wearing shoes, but the asphalt was too hot for bare feet and the shoulder was glittering with broken glass. While they waited for the bus, 72 lifted his shirt to wipe his face with it, and she saw a long trail of sweat tracking down the smoothness of his stomach and disappearing beneath the waistband of his pants. It did not disgust her.

When the number 12 came, 72 was obviously proud, at least, to be able to read the number – he nearly shouted it. But once they boarded, they learned they'd have to have a ticket. They had to get off the bus again and return inside, where the man behind the ticket desk shouted at them for holding up the line, for struggling with their dollars and giving over the wrong bills, and Lyra got flustered and spilled coins all over the floor. She was too embarrassed to pick the money up – everyone was staring at her, everyone *knew* – and instead, once they'd gotten their tickets, she and 72 hurried back outside despite people calling after them. But the bus had gone and they had to wait for a new one. Mercifully, the bus that arrived was mostly empty, so Lyra and 72 could get a seat in the back, far from the other passengers.

It was better to ride in a bus than in a car. It made her less nauseous. But still the world outside her window seemed to go by with dizzying speed, and there was ever more of it: highways rising up over new towns and then falling away into other highways; stretches of blank land burned by the sun into brownness; building and building and building, like an endless line of teeth. After an hour she spotted a monstrous coil of plastic rising into the air, twisting and snakelike and vivid blue, and an enormous billboard tacked into the ground announced *Bluefin* and *Water Park*, and several other words between them she didn't have time to read.

They passed a parking lot glittering with cars and people, natural humans: children brown from the sun, only half-dressed and carting colorful towels, men and women herding them toward the entrance. She saw a mother crouching in front of a girl red in the face from crying, touching her face with a tissue – but the bus was moving too quickly and soon a line of trees ran across her vision, obscuring it.

The driver announced Palm Grove and stopped the bus in front of a run-down motel named the Starlite. Lyra had been imagining a grid of houses in pastel shades, like the neighborhood they'd left in the middle of the night. But Palm Grove was big: big roads with two lanes of traffic, restaurants and gas stations, clothing stores and places to buy groceries. Signs shouted at them from every corner. *Milk, 3.99. Guys and Dolls, Albert Irving Auditorium, Saturday. One-Hour Parking Monday through Saturday.* She didn't even see any houses, and she counted at least a dozen people on the streets, passing in and out of shops, talking on phones. It was so hot it felt like being inside a body, beneath the skin of something, filmy and slick. How many humans could possibly be here, in one town?

'And now what?' 72 said. He'd been in a bad mood all morning, ever since she had asked him why he had the scars on his forearms, which were different from the scars she and the other replicas had, the ones from spinal taps and harvesting procedures – all of it, she knew now, to test how deep the prions had gone, how fast they were cloning themselves, how soon the replicas would die.

He had only said *accident*, and had barely spoken to her on the bus. Instead he had sat with his chin on his chest, his arms folded, his eyes shut. She had counted fourteen scars, four on his right and ten on his left. She had noticed a small mole on his earlobe, had felt a secret thrill at sitting so close after years of seeing no male replicas at all.

'Trust me,' Lyra said, which was what the nurses always said. *Shhh. Trust me. Just a little pinch. Stop with that noise. Trust me, it'll all be over soon.*

Lyra worked up the courage to stop the first person she saw who looked to be about her age. The girl was sitting on the curb in front of a store called Digs and was bent over her cell phone, typing on it. When she looked up, Lyra saw that she was wearing makeup and was vaguely surprised – she'd somehow thought makeup was for older humans, like the nurses. 'Hello,' she said. 'We're looking for Emily Huang.'

'Emily Huang.' The girl looked Lyra up and down, and then her eyes went to 72. She straightened up, giving him a smile that reminded Lyra of the actresses the nurses used to watch on TV and look at in magazines they left lying around sometimes. Lyra didn't like it, and she was for the first time aware of the difference between her body and this girl's. This girl was all curves and prettiness, all smooth skin and beautiful solidity and long, flowing hair. Lyra, in her drab clothing and her sharp bones and the scar above her eyebrow, thought of that word again, *ugly*. 'Emily Huang,' the girl repeated. 'She go to Wallace?'

'I – I don't think so.' Lyra suddenly wished they hadn't stopped.

'Sorry.' The girl *did* look sorry, but she kept her eyes

on 72. 'Don't know her.' Then she turned and gave Lyra a smile that wasn't friendly – more like she'd just eaten something she shouldn't have. 'Cool scalp, by the way. Dig the Cancer Kid look.'

They went on. Lyra could still feel the girl staring and wondered if 72 did, too. All he said was, 'Too many people,' and she nodded because her throat was too tight to speak. *Ugly*. Which meant the other girl was *pretty*. What a strange way to live, among all these people – it made Lyra feel small, even less important, than she had among the thousands of replicas grown like crops in the barracks.

The next person she stopped was older and *ugly*: wrinkles that made it look as if her face was melting, pouchy bits of skin waggling under her chin. But she didn't know who Emily Huang was and only shook her head and moved off. They stopped a man, and a boy about twelve who rode a flat thing fitted with wheels that Lyra remembered only belatedly was called a skateboard. No one knew Emily Huang, and Lyra didn't like the look the man gave them.

She was hot and thirsty and losing hope. The town kept expanding. Every time they came to the end of a block she saw a new street branching off it with more buildings and more people.

'We're never going to find her,' 72 said, and she disliked the fact that he sounded happy about it, as if he'd proven a point. 'We might as well keep walking.'

'Just hold on,' she said. 'Hold on.' Spots of color floated up in front of her vision. Her T-shirt clung to her back. She took a step and found the pavement floated up to meet her. She grabbed hold of a street sign – *Loading Dock, No Standing* – to keep from falling.

'Hey.' 72's voice changed. His arm skimmed her elbow. 'Are you all right?'

'Hot,' she managed to say.

'Come on,' he said. 'With me. You need water. And shade.'

Almost directly across the street was a park that reminded her of the courtyard at Haven, down to the statue standing at its center. This one was of a woman, though, her hands held together in prayer, her head bowed. Tall trees cast the lawns in shade, and benches lined the intersecting pathways. 72 kept a hand on her elbow even though she insisted he didn't need to.

She did feel better once she'd taken a drink of water from a water fountain and found a bench in the shade where she could rest for a bit. Somewhere in the branches birds twittered out messages to one another. It was pretty here, peaceful. The park ran up to an enormous redbrick building, portions of its facade encased in glossy sheets of climbing ivy. Lyra saw another cross stuck above the glass double doors and the letters beside it: Wallace High

School. Her heart jumped. Wallace. The girl on the street had mentioned Wallace.

'What do you want to do now?' 72 was being extra nice, which made Lyra feel worse. She knew he thought they'd failed. She knew he knew how sick she was. Without answering him, she stood up. She'd just seen someone moving behind the glass doors, and she went forward as if drawn by the pull of something magnetic. 'Lyra!' 72 shouted after her. But she didn't stop. It didn't take him long to catch up with her, but by then she was already standing in front of Wallace and a woman had emerged, carrying a stack of folders.

'Can I help you?' the woman said, and Lyra realized she'd been standing there staring.

'We're looking for Emily Huang,' Lyra said quickly, before she could lose her nerve. Remembering what the girl had said, Lyra added, 'We think – she may *go* to Wallace.' She wasn't sure what that meant, either, and she held her breath, hoping the woman did.

The woman slid on a pair of glasses, which she was wearing on a chain. Blinking up at Lyra, she resembled a turtle, down to the looseness of the skin around her neck.

'Emily Huang,' the woman said, shaking her head. 'No, no. She never went here.' Lyra's heart dropped. Another *no*. Another dead end. But then the woman said, 'But she came every career day to talk to the kids about the work she did. Terrible some of the stuff they said about her later. She was a good girl. I liked her very much.'

'So you know her?' Lyra said. She was dizzy with sudden joy. Nurse Em. She would help. She would protect them. 'You know where we can find her?'

The woman gave her a look Lyra couldn't quite read. 'Knew her,' she said slowly. 'She lived right over on Willis Street, just behind the school. Can't miss it. A sweet yellow house, and all those flower beds. Woman who lives there now has let it go to seed.'

And just like that, the happiness was gone. Evaporated. 'She's gone?' Lyra said. 'Do you know where she went?'

The woman shook her head again, and then Lyra did know how to name her expression: *pity*. 'Not gone, honey,' she said. 'Never left, some say. Hung herself right there in her living room, must be three, four years ago now. Emily Huang's dead.'

Lyra didn't know what made her want to see the place where Emily Huang had lived. When she asked for directions to Willis Street, 72 didn't question her, and she was glad. She wouldn't have known how to explain.

Behind the school they found quiet residential streets running like spokes away from the downtown, and houses at last, these concealed not behind walls but standing there pleasantly right on their lawns, with flowers waving from flower boxes and vivid toys scattered in the grass. It was pretty here, and she couldn't imagine why Emily Huang would have been so unhappy, why she would have killed herself like poor Pepper had. Then again, she remembered how Nurse Em had sobbed and Dr. O'Donnell had held her by the shoulders. *I know you,* she'd said. *You're a good person. I know you were just in over your head.* So maybe she was unhappy even then.

Nurse Em's old house had once, the old woman had told them, been the yellow of sunshine and thus easy to spot. Now it was a faded color that reminded Lyra of mustard. The flower beds looked scraggly, and there were four bikes dumped on the front lawn and so many toys it looked as if these were coming up from the ground. Loud music came to them across the lawn.

She closed her eyes and arranged all her memories of Nurse Em in a row: Nurse Em bathing Lyra and a dozen other replicas when they were too young to do it themselves, plunging them into the bathwater and hauling them like slippery, wriggling puppies onto the cold tile floor afterward. Nurse Em standing with Dr. Saperstein in the courtyard, speaking in a low voice, and the way he said, 'It's nothing. They don't understand,' after Nurse Em turned around and caught Lyra staring; the time in the janitor's closet with Dr. O'Donnell.

'I'm sorry,' 72 said, and Lyra opened her eyes. Maybe

he wasn't angry at her anymore. His eyes were softened with color.

It was the first time anyone had ever apologized to her. 'For what?'

'I know you were hoping she would help,' 72 said.

'Now we have no one,' Lyra said. She pressed a hand to her eyes. She didn't want 72 to see how upset she was. 'Nowhere to go, either.'

72 hesitated. He touched the back of her hand. 'You have me,' he said very quietly. She looked up at him, surprised. Her skin tingled where he touched her.

'I do?' she said. She felt hot in her head and chest, but it was a good feeling, like standing in the sun after being too long in the air-conditioning.

He nodded. 'You have me,' he said. 'I have you.'

He looked as if he might say more, but just then in the house next to Emily Huang's the garage door rattled open, revealing an enormously fat woman in a tracksuit. She waddled out dragging a trash bin, keeping her eyes on 72 and Lyra. Lyra stepped from him. She felt as if they'd been caught in the middle of something, even though they'd just been standing there. She waited for the woman to turn around and return inside, but instead she just stood there at the end of the driveway, one hand on the trash bin, breathing hard and staring.

'You need something?' she called out to them, when

she had caught her breath. She pulled her T-shirt away from her skin. A large sweat stain had darkened between her breasts.

'No,' 72 said quickly.

But the woman kept staring at them, and so Lyra added, 'We came looking for Emily Huang. We were . . . friends.' She enjoyed the way the word sounded and felt like repeating it, but bit her tongue so she wouldn't.

The woman's face changed, became narrower, as if she were speaking to them through a half-open door. 'You knew Emily?'

Lyra had never had to lie so much in her life. She wondered if lying, too, was a human trait. She fumbled for an excuse, and for a second her brain turned up nothing but white noise. What was the word again? 'Parents,' she said finally. It came to her like a match striking. 'She was friends with my – our – parents.'

Even 72 turned to look at her. Her cheeks were hot. This lie felt different, heavier. The word, *parents*, had left a thick feeling in her throat, as if it had slugged its way up from her stomach. She was sure that the woman would know that she was lying. But instead she just made a desperate flapping motion. It wasn't until 72 moved that Lyra realized the woman was gesturing them forward.

'In.' She had a funny, duck-like walk. She kept turning around to see that they were following her. 'Come on.

Come *on*.' Lyra didn't have enough experience to wonder whether it was safe to follow a stranger into her house, and soon they were standing in the coolness of the garage and the door was grinding closed behind them, like an eyelid squeezing shut and wedging out all the light. The garage smelled faintly of fertilizer and chemicals.

'Sorry for being a push,' the woman said, moving to a door that must, Lyra knew, connect with the house. 'You never know who's watching around here. Nosy Nellies, that's what everyone is. That was Em's problem, you ask me. Trusted all the wrong people.' She opened the door. 'I'm Sheri, by the way. Sheri Hayes. Come on in and have a chat with me. You kids look like you could use a lemonade or a bite to eat.'

Lyra and 72 didn't look at each other, but she knew what he was thinking: these real-humans were not like the ones at Haven. They were nice. Helpful. Then again, they didn't know what Lyra and 72 really were. Lyra had a feeling that they wouldn't be quite so helpful then. She imagined the inside of her body rotted, filled with disease, and wondered if soon it would begin to show on her outside, in the look of her face.

'Well, come on. Don't just stand there gawping. I'm sweating buckets.'

They followed the woman – Sheri – into the house. Lyra was startled by a cat that streaked across the hall directly in front of her, and jumped back.

'Oh, you're not allergic, are you? I've got three of 'em. Tabby, Tammy, Tommy. All littermates. Little terrors, every last one. But don't worry, they won't bite you.'

Lyra saw another two cats perched on a sofa in a darkened living room, their eyes moon-bright and yellow. Her heart was still hammering. She wasn't used to animals roaming *free* like that. At Haven the animals were kept in cages. She was glad they went instead into the kitchen.

Sheri sat them down at a wooden table and brought them two glasses of lemonade in tall glasses filled to the rim with ice cubes. It was delicious. She laid out cookies, too, a whole plate of them.

'So where do you kids come from?' Sheri asked, and Lyra froze, caught off guard again. 72 moved his thumb over a knot in the table. But Sheri just made a kind of clucking noise. 'I see,' she said. 'Let me guess. Emily helped place you with your parents, didn't she? You went through the Home Foundation?'

Lyra didn't know what she was talking about so she stayed quiet, and Sheri seemed to take that for a yes.

''Course she did. You two don't look a lick alike.' She sighed. 'Poor Emily. You knew her well, then?'

'In a way,' Lyra said carefully. She knew Nurse Em had never hit the replicas, or cursed them for being demons. She knew that Dr. O'Donnell thought she was a good person who wanted to make things right. She knew she'd been younger than many of the other nurses, because she'd overheard Dr. O'Donnell say that, too. *You're young. You didn't know what you were doing. No one will blame you.*

'She was a good girl. All that work she did for other people. I could have killed them for what they said about her in the papers after she died. It came as a shock to me, you know, a real shock. We'd been talking about a barbecue that very weekend. She called me the day it happened, asked if I wanted macaroni salad or potato.' Sheri shook her head. 'Now what kind of person about to hang herself is worried about macaroni or potato salad?'

Lyra knew she wasn't expected to answer. Sheri went on. 'Too sad. She was still young, too. Thirty-four, thirty-five. I think there must have been a man involved. Maybe more than one. Well, I suppose there were signs. You know, after they found her body I did a little bit of Googling. Found out some of the warning signs. Of course, I didn't see them before. But she did give away some of her things the week before she died, and that's right up there to look for. Giving away prized possessions. Of course at the time I thought she was just being nice.'

'What do you mean, there was a man involved?' 72 asked, and Lyra was surprised, as ever, to hear him speak. She realized he hardly spoke unless they were alone.

Somehow, this made her feel special. Her glass was empty but still cold, and she pressed it to her neck.

'Well, isn't there always?' She raised her eyebrows. 'Besides, it would've been hard not to notice those men in and out. Just once or twice, of course, as far as I could tell. Suited-up types. Like in finance or something. But mean-looking.' Lyra thought of the Suits who'd come to inspect Haven sometimes and felt a curious prickling down the back of her spine. *Those men.* Like the nurses had always called them. Sheri shook her head. 'But there's no accounting for taste, I always say.'

Lyra grasped for some idea of what to ask next, of what any of this meant or whether it mattered. 'You said she was giving away her things,' she said, suddenly struck by what this might mean. 'She gave *you* something, didn't she?' Lyra asked. Maybe, she thought, Nurse Em had left Sheri something important – maybe she'd left her something that related to Haven and to the work they were doing there. To the prions.

To a cure.

Sheri had taken a seat. Now she placed both palms on the table to stand up. 'Never been able to find a place for them. But can't bring myself to throw 'em out, either. Oh, she told me I could. Told me I could take the damn things apart and sell the frames, if I wanted. But of course I never would.' She moved off into another room. 72 gave Lyra a questioning look and she shrugged. She didn't know what she was waiting for or looking for anymore. Only that out there, in the real world, there were no answers – nothing but vastness and things she'd never seen in real life and experiences she couldn't understand and strangers who didn't know what she was and would hate her if they did. Nothing but the disease. Nothing but being nothing and then dying nothing.

At Haven she'd never *wanted* anything, not in any way that counted. She'd been hungry, tired, bored, and sick. She'd wanted more food, cold water, more sleep, for the pain to end, to go outside. But she'd never had a want that moved her, where the goal felt not like an end but a beginning. She'd never had a purpose. But now she did. She wanted to understand.

And this single fact made her feel more human, more *worthy*, than she ever had before.

She was shocked to feel 72's hand in hers. She looked up at him and felt the same strange thing happen to her body, as if she was transformed to air. He pulled away when Sheri returned to the room, carrying three framed photographs. She plunked them down on the table.

'Well, you see, they're not exactly my taste,' Sheri said. The pictures were all illustrations. Lyra guessed they came from the same anatomy textbook. She'd seen many similar pictures in the medical textbooks at Haven. 'I like my kittens and my watercolors and oils here and there. Never been much for drawing.'

Lyra thought the drawings were beautiful – she loved the sinewy look of the muscles, the precision of the bones, and even the faded lettering too small to make out, labeling different physical features. But even so, she was horribly disappointed. There was nothing here, no secret message or miracle cure.

Somewhere in the house, a phone rang. Sheri stood up again. 'It never ends, does it?' she said. 'Give me just a minute.' As soon as she left, another cat, this one gray, leapt onto the table, and Lyra instinctively grabbed one of the framed illustrations to keep the cat from stepping on it.

'Why have cats in a house?' 72 whispered to her. But she couldn't answer, even though she'd been wondering the same thing. She'd felt an irregularity in the canvas backing, and she flipped the frame over, her chest suddenly cavernous with hope.

The canvas had at one time been stapled to the wooden frame. On two sides of the rectangular canvas, the staples were in place. But on two sides they were missing, and instead had been replaced with gobs of glue at inch-long intervals, some of which had seeped out and hardened onto the wood. Lyra and the other replicas had spent too long at Haven searching for places to hide their limited belongings not to suspect that the picture Nurse Em had given Sheri was in fact concealing something else behind it.

Nurse Em had told Sheri she could *take the damn things apart*. What if she had meant that Sheri *should* take the damn things apart?

The phone had stopped ringing, and Sheri's voice, muffled by the walls, was now nothing more than tones. She must have closed a door. Before she could lose her nerve, Lyra pried a corner of the canvas from the frame and ripped.

'What are you doing?' 72 reached out and seized Lyra's wrist as if to stop her.

'Nurse Em gave these pictures away before she died,' Lyra whispered. 'Maybe she was hiding something.' Fearing both that she would find something and that she wouldn't, she slipped a hand behind the canvas. Almost immediately, her fingers landed on several loose items, glossy-slick. Photographs.

72 stared as she laid them out on the table. There were three of them, each showing Nurse Em with a tall, dark-haired man who had a beard and a sour expression. In one photograph, Nurse Em was sitting on his lap and he was turning away from the camera. In another, she was kissing him on the cheek and he was lifting a hand as if to block them from the lens. But in the last one she'd caught

him square on, or someone else had. They were standing in front of a nondescript stretch of highway. There was a scruffy range of blue hills in the distance. She was holding on to a straw hat and looked happy. Lyra felt sick for reasons she couldn't say.

'Dr. Saperstein,' 72 said, naming him first. Lyra could only nod. The man in the pictures was unmistakably Dr. Saperstein, whom Lyra had always thought of a little like the humans thought about their God: someone remote and all-powerful, someone through whom the whole world was ordered.

Lyra could no longer hear Sheri talking. But after a minute, there was a quick burst of laughter from the other room and she knew they still had a little time.

'Quick,' she said. 'Help me check the other frames.'

She flipped over the second picture. Like the first, its backing had been pulled away from the frame and then reglued. But this one had been done more carefully and was difficult to detach. 72 leaned across her, knife in hand, and neatly sliced the canvas, barely missing her fingers.

'It's faster,' he said, and leaned across her to slit open the back of the third picture.

They found, behind the second picture, a folded sheet of paper that looked at first glance to be a list of names and a typed document, although Lyra didn't have time to try and read it. She didn't have time to check the third picture frame, either. At that moment she heard a door open, and Sheri's voice, suddenly amplified.

'I'll call you tomorrow,' she was saying. 'I'm being rude . . .'

Sheri would only have to glance at the frames to know what they had done and to guess, probably, that something had been removed from behind the pictures. Without speaking, she and 72 stood up from the table and moved as quietly as they could to the back door, which opened out onto a little patio. Sheri was still trying to get off the phone. Lyra saw her pass momentarily into view and froze, one hand on the door handle.

'I have *guests*,' Sheri was saying. 'But I was listening, I promise . . .'

Then Sheri, who was pacing, passed out of view again without looking up.

Lyra eased open the screen door, wincing when it squeaked on its hinges. 72 ducked outside onto the stone patio. One of the cats was still staring at her, unblinkingly, and for a terrifying second Lyra thought it might open its mouth and let out a wail of alarm.

But it made not a sound, and so Lyra slipped after 72, closing the door behind her.

THIRTEEN

LYRA HALF EXPECTED SHERI TO come running after them, and they were several blocks away before she thought that they were probably safe. They found another park, with several dirty sandboxes and a rusted swing set at its center. But there were trees here, and shade, and they were alone.

She examined the pictures again, one by one. She'd seen romance on the nurses' televisions, of course, and heard the staff at Haven talk about boyfriends and girlfriends and wives and husbands. She knew about it. But knowing about what humans did, the kinds of relationships they had on TV, was different from seeing and holding proof of this. Dr. Saperstein had struck her not so much as human but as some bloodless stone deity come to life. She had never once seen him smile. True, he wasn't smiling in these pictures, either, but he was dressed in T-shirts and striped shorts and a baseball hat, like he could have been anybody. This made him more frightening to her, not less. She thought of the snakes at Haven that left their long, golden skins on the ground, brittle and husk-like.

Nurse Em was hardly recognizable. She looked so happy. Lyra thought again of the last time she'd seen her – sobbing into Dr. O'Donnell's arms. And she had killed herself, using a rope instead of a knife, as Pepper had.

What had happened?

Sheri had mentioned men in suits visiting Nurse Em before she died. Was Dr. Saperstein one of them? Before looking at the photographs, Lyra had never seen him in anything but a lab coat.

She unfolded the list. 72 leaned over her. He smelled sweet, as if he was sweating soap. 'What does it say?' he asked impatiently, and she had the sudden, ridiculous urge to take his hand, to tuck herself into the space between his arm and shoulder, as Nurse Em and Dr. Saperstein were doing in the picture.

She read instead thirty-four names – all names she didn't know, nobody she recognized from Haven – in alphabetical order. Donald Bartlett. Caroline Ciao. Brandy-Nicole Harliss. She stopped. That name seemed somehow familiar, and yet she couldn't think why. But rereading it gave her the weirdest sensation, like when the doctors used to bang her on the knee to test her reflexes and she would see her body jerk. Like something inside of her was *stirring*.

The second piece of paper, Lyra had trouble deciphering at first. It wasn't a list, but a full page of writing, and it picked up in the middle of a sentence. As Lyra began to read, she had the impression that Nurse Em was talking to *her*, to an invisible other body that existed beyond the page.

. . . eggs on my car, it began. Lyra read the phrase several times, trying to make sense of it, before she decided there must have been a first sheet that had gotten lost. She kept reading, and both because it was easier for her to spell the words out and 72 was getting impatient, she read slowly, out loud.

"'Mark tells me not to worry so much. I know they're kooks'" – Lyra stumbled a little over the word, since she'd never heard it – "'but they aren't that far off. Someone stopped me the other day after I caught the ferry. They're raising zombies, aren't they? she said. A normal woman. Someone you'd see at the grocery store.' She continued reading.

> *It gave me chills, Ellen. I felt for a second as if she knew. Is it really so different, after all?*
>
> *I tell you, I never thought I'd miss Philadelphia. I don't miss the winters, that's for sure. But I miss you, Elbow, and*

I miss how simple things felt back then. I even miss that shitty apartment we found through Drexel — remember? — and that stupid ex-boyfriend of yours who used to throw cans at your window. Ben? Sometimes I even miss our coursework (!!). At least I felt like we were on the right path.

I know what you'll say. It's the same thing Mark says. And I believe in the science, I do. If a parent loses a child . . . well, to have that child back . . . Who wouldn't want that? Who wouldn't try? When I think of people like Geoffrey Ives . . . All the money in the world and a dead baby that he couldn't save and all he wants is to make it better. To undo it.

But is it right? Mark thinks so. But I don't know. I can't decide. Dr. Haven wants to keep the NIH out of our hair, so he stays clear of dealing with the clinics, even though they've got fetal tissue they'll sell off for just the transportation fee. But already the funds are running thin. I don't think there's any way we'll last unless we get federal support, but if good old George W. outlaws spending on the research. . . .

Then there's the question of Dr. Haven. Ever since he went into AA, he's been changing. Mark worries he'll shut down the program, shut down the whole institution. He doesn't seem to be sure, at least not anymore, and if the donors' money dries up, we'll have to go in a totally new direction. Mark thinks there might be other ways, military research, cures —

The writing stopped. Lyra flipped over the page, but there was nothing more. She'd either been interrupted or the rest of what she'd said had been lost. Lyra also assumed from the reference to an Ellen, a name, that Nurse Em must have been intending the message for someone specific. She had never passed it on. But she'd felt it was important enough to hide – to hide well – and to deliver to someone before she died.

Was she hoping Sheri would find it?

What was Nurse Em hoping she'd see?

It was a puzzle. It was data. It was a *code,* like DNA was.

All codes could be read, if you only knew the key.

For a long minute, she and 72 stood there in silence, in the shadow of a construction of wood and rope and plastic whose purpose she didn't know. Codes everywhere. That was the problem with the outside world, the human world. The whole thing was made up of puzzles, of a language she didn't quite speak.

'What does it mean?' 72 asked finally, and she realized that that was the question: about standing in the park, about him and his moods and the way he sometimes rubbed the back of his neck as if something was bothering him there, about their escape and the fact that they were dying anyway but she didn't feel like she was dying. She didn't feel like dying.

What does it mean?

She had never asked that question.

She forced herself to reread, squinting, as if she could squeeze more meaning from the letters that way. She knew that Haven made replicas from human tissue, and she knew, of course, that it must have come from humans, people. She knew there were hospitals and clinics that did business with Haven, although she didn't know how she knew this, exactly. It was just a fact of life, like the cots and the Stew Pot and *failure to thrive*.

And she knew what zombies were. The nurses had talked about them, about several zombie movies and how scary they were. Lyra explained what they were to 72 but he, too, had heard of them. The human world – or at least some of it – had penetrated Haven.

'Read it out loud again,' he said, and she did, conscious all the time of the sun on the back of her neck and 72 and his smell and that question – *what does it mean?* – all of it shimmering momentarily and so present and also so insubstantial, like something on fire, hot and at the same time burning into nonexistence.

She took her time with the sentences she thought were most important.

> . . . *he stays clear of dealing with the clinics, even though they've got fetal tissue they'll sell off for just the transportation fee* . . .

When I think of people like Geoffrey Ives . . .

All the money in the world and a dead baby that he couldn't save . . .

And finally she understood.

'Dead children,' Lyra said. *Zombies. Is it so different?* 'They were making replicas from dead children.' Was that how she'd been made? From the tissue of a child who'd been loved, grieved over, and lost? It shouldn't have made a difference and yet it did, somehow. It wasn't even the fact that the children had died as much as the fact that at one time they'd been cared for.

And yet the process of making their doubles – the *science* of it – had turned Lyra and the other replicas into something different. She remembered how sometimes the voices of the protesters had carried over on the wind, across the miles of snaggletoothed marshes. *Monsters,* they'd shouted.

But for the first time Lyra felt not shame, but anger. She hadn't asked to be made. She'd been brought into the world a monster and then hated for it, and it wasn't her fault, and there was no meaning behind that.

None at all.

'It doesn't make sense,' 72 said. 'Why kill us, then?'

'Something changed,' Lyra said. She could hardly remember Dr. Haven. She may have seen him once or twice. She could vividly recall his face, but then again she'd seen pictures of him her whole life: Dr. Haven in oils staring down at them from the framed painting at the end of the mess hall, Dr. Haven in black and white, pictured squinting into the sun in front of G-Wing.

They stood there again in silence. Had Lyra been intended originally for the human parents of a child who had died? But if so, why had they never come for her? Maybe they had, but found the substitute terrible.

Maybe they hadn't been able to stomach looking at her – the flimsy substitute for the girl they'd loved and had to grieve.

'She mentions a cure,' 72 said quietly. 'Maybe you were right. Maybe she did know something that could help us.'

'Well, she's dead now,' Lyra said. Her voice sounded hollow, as if she were speaking into a cup.

'Lyra.' 72 touched her elbow, and she pulled away from him. His touch burned, *physically* burned, although she knew that was impossible. His skin was no hotter than anyone else's. She turned away from him, blinking hard, and for a second, looking out across the park and to the houses in the distance – all those parents, families, moms and dads – she transformed the afternoon sun striking the windows into white flame, and imagined burning the whole world down, just like they'd burned down Haven.

'On the bus you asked me why the cuts,' 72 said. This surprised her, and she momentarily forgot her anger and turned back to look at him. His skin in the light looked like something edible, coffee and milk. 'When I was younger I didn't understand what I was. *If* I was.'

Lyra didn't have to say anything to show she understood. She had wondered the same thing. She had confused *it* for *I*, had pinched number 25 to see if she herself would feel it, because she didn't understand where she ended and the herd began.

'I started thinking maybe I wasn't real. And then I started worrying that I wasn't, that I was disappearing. I used to . . .' He swallowed and rubbed his forehead, and Lyra realized with a sudden thrill she *knew* what he was feeling: he was scared. She had read him.

'It's okay,' she said automatically.

'I got hold of one of the doctor's scalpels once,' he said, in a sudden rush. 'I kept it in my mattress, took out some of the stuffing so that no one would find it.' Lyra thought of the hole in Ursa Major's mattress, and all the things they'd found stashed inside of it. She thought, too, of how Ursa had just stood there and screamed while her mattress was emptied – one high, shrill note, like the cresting of an alarm. 'I used to have to check. I felt better when I saw the blood. I knew I was still alive, then.' He raised his eyes to hers, and in her chest she had a lifting, swooping sensation, as if something heavy had come loose. 'You wanted to know. So I'm telling you.'

She didn't know what to say. So she said, 'Thank you.' She reached out and moved her finger from his elbow all the way to his wrist, over the ridge of his scars, to show him it was okay, and that she understood. She could feel him watching her. She could *feel* him, everywhere he was, as if he was distorting the air, making it heavier.

She had never *felt* so much in her life.

'We'll go back,' 72 said, so quietly she nearly missed it.

'Back?' she repeated. He was standing so close she was suddenly afraid and took a step away from him.

'The girl, Gemma. And Jake.' He hesitated. 'You were right all along. They might be able to help. They know about Haven. Maybe they'll know about a cure, too.'

'But . . .' She shook her head. 'You said you didn't trust them.'

'I don't,' he said simply. 'But I don't trust anyone.'

'Even me?' Lyra asked.

Something changed in his eyes. 'You're different,' he said, in a softer voice.

'Why?' She was aware of how close they were, and of the stillness of the afternoon, all the trees bound and silent.

He almost smiled. He reached up. He pressed a thumb

to her lower lip. His skin tasted like salt. 'Because we're the same.'

Lyra knew they'd never be able to backtrack. They'd left the house in the middle of the night and they'd hardly been paying attention – they'd been thinking of nothing but escape – and she could remember no special feature of the house to which they'd been taken, nothing to distinguish it from its neighbors.

Fortunately, 72 remembered that Jake had written down his address and phone number. They couldn't call – 72 had stolen Jake's phone, and besides, Lyra had never made a call before and, though she had often seen the nurses talking on their cell phones, wasn't sure she knew how to do it – and so they started the process again of asking strangers how to get to 1211 Route 12, Little Waller, Florida.

A woman with hair frosted a vague orange color directed them to a car rental agency, but almost as soon as they entered, the man behind the counter began asking for licenses and credit cards and other things neither one of them had. Lyra got flustered again, upsetting a small display of maps with her elbow so the maps went fanning out across the counter. 72 got angry. He accused the man of shouting.

'I barely raised my voice,' the man said. 'You some kinda freak or something?'

Quickly, 72 reached for his pocket, and Lyra was

worried he was going for his knife. The man must have been worried, too, because he stumbled backward, toppling his chair. But instead 72 just put the paper with Jake's address onto the desk.

'You have a map,' he said. His voice was low and tight, as if the words were bound together with wire. 'Show us how to get here. *Please.*'

The man reached for a map slowly, keeping his eyes on 72. A TV in the corner reeled off the sound of an audience laughing, but otherwise it was so quiet that Lyra could hear the man's lungs, like something wet caught in his chest as he took a red pen, pointed out the different bus routes they could take to reach Little Waller, less than an hour away. Lyra noticed his hand was shaking ever so slightly – and for the first time the idea of being a *freak*, of being a *monster*, made her feel not ashamed but powerful.

There were only two other passengers on the bus, including a man wearing several different layers of clothing who smelled like sweat and urine. Lyra and 72 took a seat at the very back. They sat so close their thighs and knees touched, and Lyra felt the warmth coming through the window like the gentle pressure of a hand. As the bus passed the water park, Lyra pressed her nose to the window, eager again for the sight of all those real human families. But the sun was hard in her eyes and she could see nothing but blurred, indistinct figures.

Then they were on the highway again, passing long stretches of vivid green space where there were no towns or houses, just trees crowning the roads, just growth and dark spaces.

72 was quiet for so long, leaning back with his eyes closed, she thought he'd fallen asleep. But then he turned to face her. The sunlight fell across his skin and made it seem to glow. When he spoke, she felt his breath on her ear and in her hair. 'Can I ask you a question about your story?' he said. 'About the little prince, and the rose?'

'Okay.' Lyra took a breath. She again had a sense of his whole body extended there in space, the miracle of all those interwoven molecules that kept him together.

His eyes were dark, and she could see herself inside of them. 'You said the Little Prince lived on Planet B-612,' he said. 'You pointed it out to me.' He bit his lip and she had the strangest desire to bite it too, to feel his lips with her mouth. 'But all the stars look the same. So how do you know?'

'Not if you look closely,' she said. Her body was bright hot, burning. It was his breath on her shoulder and the feel of him next to her in the afternoon sun. 'That's what the Little Prince found too, on his travels. He thought his rose was the only rose in the whole universe at first. But then he came down to earth and found a garden of them.'

72 shifted and their knees touched again. The sun

made his eyes dazzle, and the rest of the world was disappearing. 'What happened then?'

She tried to remember the rest of the story. It was hard to concentrate with him so close. She kept imagining his skin under his clothing, and beneath his skin, his organs and ribs and the blood alive in his veins, kept thinking of this miracle, that he should exist, that they both should, instead of just being empty space. But what came to her was Dr. O'Donnell's voice, and the way she'd leaned forward to read this part of the book, her dirty-blond hair falling out from where it was tucked behind her ears.

'He was very sad,' Lyra said slowly. 'He thought the rose had tricked him. She wasn't special. She was just like thousands of other roses. Identical to them,' she added.

'A replica,' 72 said.

'Exactly,' Lyra said, although it was the first time she'd made the connection, and understood, truly understood, why Dr. O'Donnell had given her that particular book. 'Just like a replica. Only . . .'

'What?'

'Only the Little Prince realized his rose was special. She was the only one in the universe. Because he'd cared for her, and talked with her, and protected her from caterpillars. She was *his* rose. And that made her more special than all the other roses in the universe combined.' Lyra found the sun was painful and blinked. She was crying.

She turned away and brought a hand to her face quickly, hoping 72 wouldn't see.

But he caught her hand. And before she could ask what he was doing, before she could even be afraid, her body responded. It knew what to do. It sensed a question and answered for her, so she found herself turning to face him, placing her hand against his face so the warmth of him spread through her fingers. They sat there, looking at each other, on a bus suspended in space. She knew it was impossible, but she thought her heart stopped beating completely.

'Lyra,' he whispered.

'What?' she whispered back. His face was cut into geometric shapes by shadows, and he was a beautiful puzzle to her, mysterious and ever-changing.

But he didn't answer. He brought his fingers to her face. He touched her cheekbones and her forehead and the bridge of her nose. 'Lyra,' he said again. 'I like your name.' Then: 'I wish I had a name.'

Lyra closed her eyes. He kept touching her. He ran his fingers across her scalp. He traced the long curve of her earlobe, and then moved a finger down her neck, pressing lightly as though to feel her pulse beating up through his hand. And everywhere he touched, she imagined she was healed. She imagined the disease simply vanishing, evaporating, like water under the sun. 'We can give you a name,' she said, still with her eyes closed. 'You can take one from the stars, like I did.'

He was quiet for a while. His hand moved to her shoulder. He walked his fingers along her collarbone. He placed his thumb in the hollow of her throat.

'You pick,' he said, and for the briefest second he touched her lips, too. Then he placed his hand flat against her chest, just above her heart.

In the darkness behind her eyelids she saw a universe explode into being, expand into brightness. She pictured names and stars bright blue or purple or white-hot.

'Caelum,' she said. She knew it was right as soon as she said it out loud. 'You'll be Caelum.'

'Caelum,' he repeated. Even without opening her eyes, she could tell he was smiling.

FOURTEEN

SOMETHING HAD CHANGED. LYRA COULDN'T have said what it was, exactly, only that something had softened in Caelum, or in her, or both. They were bound together. They had chosen each other, to be responsible for and to care for each other.

By four p.m. they had reached Little Waller, although Lyra asked several people to be sure. A policeman spotted them standing at a corner, puzzling over the sign, and came loping down the street. Lyra's chest tightened – he was wearing a uniform similar to the one the guards had worn at Haven, and she thought of that night on the marshes and how the soldiers had been afraid to move Cassiopeia, afraid she might be contagious. *You know how expensive these things are to make?* But the policeman only asked them if they needed help and pointed the way.

'Straight and keep walking,' he said. 'That road runs

right out into marshland. Couldn't have picked a nicer day for it.' She didn't know whether he was being serious. It was already so hot the pavement shimmered.

On their way through town they passed a blocky cement building called the Woodcrest Retirement Home. Behind a tall hedgerow, several sprinklers were tossing up water, crossing in midair, making shimmering rainbows. Both Lyra and Caelum crouched to drink, and Lyra felt a bit like a dog but not in a bad way. She and Caelum were a team, a pack. They could survive like this. They would survive. They'd figure out a way.

Together.

Caelum stood guard while Lyra took off her filthy shirt and her jeans, and, crouching, moved into the spray of water to clean herself. They had no towels, so she had to get dressed right away again, but it didn't matter: the water was delicious and cold, and she was happier than she could ever remember being. Then she stood watch for him, although she couldn't resist looking after he'd stripped off his shirt. She had seen anatomical drawings of the muscles connecting the shoulder blades and torqued around the spine, but she had never imagined that they could make this, something seamless and graceful. Something *beautiful*.

They set out again, their shirts damp with water, their socks squelching a little in their shoes. Neither of them cared. They walked in silence, but it wasn't uncomfortable at all. Lyra and Caelum: the two replicas with names plucked straight from the stars.

Jake's road was little more than a dirt path through the woods, crowded with tall spruce trees and hanging moss and loud with the chitter of birds. All at once Lyra felt her happiness picked apart by anxiety, by the sense of someone concealed and watching. But the road was empty except for a dead turtle, flattened under a car tire, and a bird picking at it. The bird flapped away as soon as they approached.

What was that feeling? It was standing naked in front of a team of doctors and nurses. It was the lights in the operation room, and the shadow of people moving behind glass.

Jake's house, number 1211, looked like it had simply been dropped there, temporarily stifling a nest of exploding growth. Two shutters were broken and the window boxes were empty. But a little lawn had been cleared in front of the porch, and someone had repainted the exterior yellow to conceal the moisture rotting out the baseboards. A cat slunk beneath the porch, and for a paranoid second Lyra was sure that Sheri Hayes had followed them all this way to yell at them for ruining her pictures. But that didn't make sense. And there must be many cats in the world. There were many *everything* in this world.

Lyra followed Caelum to the front door. The sun was hot on the back of her neck and felt weighty. They knocked and rang the doorbell. No one came. Jake's car was in the driveway, though. Lyra recognized it. They rang the doorbell again. Caelum leaned in to listen at the door. But it was obvious no one was home. There was not a single creak from inside.

'He must be out,' Lyra said at last, although she hated to admit it. The disappointment was almost physical. Suddenly she was exhausted again.

'We'll wait for him here, then,' Caelum said. When Lyra looked at him, he shrugged. 'He's got to be back sometime, right?'

'He said his aunt would come home today,' Lyra said. She didn't have a clear sense of what an aunt was but knew it meant family, like mother and grandmother. 'What if his aunt finds us first?'

Caelum tested the door, but it was locked. 'Come on,' he said. 'There must be another way in.'

They went around the house to the back. Here there were no signs, and no grass, either: just a small cement patio and planters filled with dying brown things, plus an old sofa, puddled with rain and specked with mildew. Sliding doors opened onto the patio and these, Lyra was relieved to find, were unlocked. At least they could wait inside, where she didn't feel so exposed.

The kitchen was a mess. There were papers scattered across the table. The drawers hung open. The refrigerator was pulled away from the wall, revealing plastic disks of insect poison behind it. Even the microwave was open. There was mail on the floor, and Lyra saw footprints where someone had walked.

'It's wrong,' Lyra said immediately.

'What is?'

'All of it.' Lyra thought about how Jake had set a napkin on the coffee table before setting down a glass of water, how he had adjusted his computer so that it ran parallel to the table edge. 'Someone else was here before us.'

Caelum looked at her. 'Or he doesn't like to pick up after himself,' he said.

'No.' Lyra shook her head. She was afraid. 'Someone was here.'

They moved from the kitchen into a small living room. This, too, was a mess. It was as if a library had exploded. Papers, folders, books. A coffee mug, overturned, pooling onto the rug. Jake's computer was on the couch, flashing a moving image – a picture of deep space, vivid with color. When Lyra touched it, the image dissolved, leaving in its place a small white box and the demand for a password. Inspired, she bent down and sought out the letters on the keyboard one by one. H–A–V–E–N. But the password was refused, and almost immediately she felt sorry. The help they needed wouldn't be found there on the computer anyway.

Caelum went out of the living room. Lyra was about to follow him when she saw several photographs displayed on a wall-mounted shelf. One of them, a portrait of Jake from when he was a kid, was framed. The other two were just stacked there, and smudgy with fingerprints.

In one of them Jake was standing next to a man she originally confused for a much older replica – they had the same dark eyes and hair, the same well-cut chin and cheekbones – but she quickly realized the man must be his father. In another, a woman with white-blond hair and breasts coming out of a tank top was grimacing at the camera, holding tight to Jake's shoulder, as if she was afraid he might run away. Was this *aunt*? It was family, she was sure of it. The woman also had Jake's square chin.

For some reason, this made her sad. Replicas were singular events. They exploded into being and they died, leaving no one. But people were just one in an interlinking series of other people.

She made a sudden decision: she would ask Caelum to be her family. That way, when she died, she wouldn't be completely alone.

In another room, Caelum shouted for her. She turned

and saw him back into the hall. In the dim light, he looked pale.

'What?' she said. 'What is it?' But she knew already.

He didn't look at her. 'Dead,' he said, with a single nod, and Lyra replaced the photographs, facedown, as if they might hear. 'Jake's dead.'

He was hanging from the closet door, just pinned there like an old suit. He'd written with black marker on one of the walls. *I'm so lonely. I can't take it anymore.* This room, the bedroom, was equally as messy as the others. A second computer was open on the bed.

Lyra had seen countless dead bodies, but this one was the first that made her want to look away. Jake Witz was no longer nice to look at. His face was purpled with blood. His tongue was exposed, stiff and dark, like something foreign that had gotten lodged there. His fingernails were broken where he had tried to free the belt, which had been wedged between the door frame and hammered in place to the far side of the door. A thick film of blood and spit had dried on his lips.

'What do you think?' Caelum asked.

'Nurse Emily hung herself, too,' Lyra said, stepping out into the hallway. A wave of dizziness overtook her, and she reached out to steady herself on a wall. Caelum followed her, and briefly put a hand on her lower back.

She wished herself back into the field last night, and their bodies silhouetted by all that darkness. 'That's what Sheri said.'

Caelum watched her. 'You don't believe it?'

She didn't know what she believed. 'Someone was here,' she repeated. She took a step toward the kitchen and stumbled. Caelum caught her elbow before she could fall. 'I'm all right,' she said, gasping a little. 'I just need to sit.'

But she felt no better sitting in Jake's kitchen and drinking water from one of his water glasses, which tasted like soap from the dishwasher. Someone had been here. Someone from Haven? They couldn't stay here. What if whoever had killed Jake came back to clean up? They needed to get to Gemma, but she had no idea how. She couldn't keep her thoughts together. They kept scattering like points of light across her vision. An alarm was going off. A beeping. She stood up. Then she saw Jake rooting through the backpack and remembered: the phone. The phone was ringing.

The phone.

'I thought you turned it off,' Caelum said.

'It must have come on again,' Lyra said. 'Here. Give it to me.' The number on the screen was labeled *Aunt Kit* and she waited, holding her breath, until the phone stopped ringing, her chest full of sharp pains. People called phones, phones called people. Would Gemma be stored in Jake's phone? Maybe. But she had no idea how to look for Gemma, how to *get* to her.

'Lyra.' Caelum's hand found her wrist. His fingers were cold. But at that moment she heard it too: footsteps outside, the muffled sound of voices. They had barely slipped into the living room before they heard the patio doors slide open and then close again. For a delirious second Lyra hoped that maybe Gemma had come for them, and thought about peeking into the kitchen to check, but when a woman spoke, her voice was unfamiliar.

'These cleanup jobs,' she said. 'I feel like a goddamn housekeeper. What exactly are we supposed to do?'

'You're looking at it. The first team left a mess. Livingston's worried someone might get suspicious. Doesn't say suicide. You're supposed to get all your shit in order, not trash the fucking place.'

'Did they find anything?'

'Don't know. The kid knew too much, though, otherwise he wouldn't be swinging from a rope.'

Sweat gathered between Lyra's breasts. She'd been right to worry that the people who killed Jake might come back. Could she and Caelum make it to the front door without being seen? They would have to pass in front of the kitchen. If the strangers were busy or had their backs turned, if they were over by the refrigerator without a clear view of the hallway, she and Caelum might manage it.

The sound of rustling papers. A chair scraping back from the table. How long would it take them to straighten up the kitchen? Not long. One of them was whistling. Lyra didn't know that people could be so casual about killing other people as they were about killing replicas. She felt something hard and hot in her throat, as if she'd swallowed an explosive. She'd been angry before, and she'd been lonely and afraid. But she had never hated, not like this.

She hated the people in the next room. She hated Dr. Saperstein. She hated the people who had killed Jake Witz, and the people who'd filled her blood with disease. She wanted to see them die.

Caelum eased off the wall, nodding to the front door. Lyra nodded back to show she understood, although she didn't really see how she would move. She was liquid fear and anger. She wanted to scream, and she could hardly stay on her feet.

Caelum moved. For a second that felt like forever, passing the entrance to the kitchen, he was exposed. It seemed to Lyra he was hanging there, hooked to the air the way Jake Witz had been hooked to the door. But then he was in the hall, and the sound of his footsteps was concealed by all the noise from the kitchen. He turned back to gesture to Lyra. *Come.*

She unstuck herself from the wall. She imagined if she turned around she would see her silhouette, all dark and sweat-discolored. On the desk Jake's computer was still flashing the picture of a beach, and then, for reasons that Lyra didn't totally understand, she was moving not toward the door but away from it. She picked up the computer, which was surprisingly light, and hugged it to her chest. She felt as if her body was making decisions and relaying them to her brain and not the other way around.

Caelum was white-faced, staring at her. She knew he wanted to scream at her to hurry up. She knew he wanted to yell *What were you thinking?* She could feel the charge of his fear in the silence.

She took a step toward the door.

The phone in her pocket, Jake's phone, began to ring.

The whole world went silent and still. In Lyra's head, a white burst of panic, a life at an end. The noise from the kitchen had completely stopped.

Then: 'What the fuck is that?'

'It's a phone.'

'No shit. Where's it coming from?'

She had no time to think. Vaguely she saw Caelum disappear, retreating down the hall. She took the phone from her pocket and tossed it on the carpet, then shimmied behind the couch, still holding Caelum's computer, as the man crossed heavily into the room. She got down on the floor, on her stomach, inhaling the smell of old upholstery and dust. When she breathed, dust stirred on the exhale. But she tried not to breathe.

She saw the man toe the cell phone with a boot. 'Aw. Look at that. Aunt Kit's calling.'

The woman's voice was now distant. She must have gone into the bedroom, or maybe the bathroom at the end of the hall. 'What'd they think, he was hiding state secrets in his porn collection? They really did a number on this place, huh?'

'You think I should snatch the phone?' The man bent down. She saw his fingers, long and a little fat. Stupidly, she felt like crying. She didn't know why, exactly. They'd stolen the phone from Jake, but now it felt like a gift, like something they were meant to have. She didn't like seeing the man's fingers on it.

'Hell no. That's the first thing the police are gonna look for. They'll know someone was here if it's gone. These kids nowadays . . .'

The man straightened up, leaving the phone, now silent again, where it was. She waited until she heard his footsteps go creaking down the hall before sliding out from behind the couch, nauseous now with fear and the nearness of her discovery. Her hand was shaking when she reached for Jake's phone, and when she stood up again she fought against a wave of blackness that nearly toppled her. She couldn't get sick now. She was almost out. Almost safe.

She took a step toward the door, and another step. She was dizzy. She reached out a hand to steady herself against the wall. The computer seemed heavier than it had only a minute ago. Her head was full of a strange buzzing, like the noise of bees.

'Aw, fuck. Now I left *my* phone –'

She barely registered the man talking again before he had stepped into the hallway and spotted her. He gave a shout – and that, his moment of surprise, of utter shock, was what saved her life. She tore her hand away from the wall and plunged across the living room, losing sight of him as she careened into the front hall.

He was shouting. The woman, too. And there were footsteps pounding after her but Lyra didn't look back, didn't stop. Caelum was at the front door. He was fumbling with the locks. He was saying something she couldn't hear. The door was open. She banged against the screen door hard with an elbow. There was a view of blue sky, of dirt and grass and exterior, and voices ringing like alarms inside her head, and then they were outside, they were out.

FIFTEEN

THEY HAD NO TIME TO do anything but duck behind a neighbor's car before they saw a dark-blue sedan edge out from Jake's driveway and nose into the street. They waited until the noise of the engine faded, then stood and started down the rutted dirt road, turning onto the next street they came to, this one thick with growth and lined with a ruin of old houses. They needed to get back to town. But Lyra was mixed up. Which way had they come?

They turned again and froze. Several blocks away, the sedan was coming toward them at a crawl. They pivoted and began to run. Lyra didn't know whether they'd been spotted and was too afraid to look. There was a roaring in her ears. The car, getting closer?

'Town.' Lyra's breath was coming in short gasps, like something alive inside her chest. 'We need to get back to town.'

She didn't know whether Caelum had heard. He made a hard right and took off straight across a front yard overgrown with high weeds. A dog began to bark, but no one came out. They squeezed into the narrow dark space between the garage and the house just as the sedan came around the corner, and looking back, Lyra saw the woman's face, white with concentration, scanning the streets through the open window. Lyra's legs were shaking so badly Caelum had to put his arms around her to keep her on her feet. His chest moved against her back, his breath was in her hair and on her neck, and she wished the world would end so she could end with it, so she didn't have to run anymore, so Caelum could stay with her in a dark, close space that felt like being buried.

But the world didn't end, of course. When the sedan was once again out of view, Caelum released her. 'Now,' he said. But she found she couldn't move. She was so tired.

'Wait. I don't think I can.'

'Okay.' Caelum looked young in the half dark, with the sky a narrow artery above them. 'We'll stay here for a bit.'

'No. I don't think I can. Go on.' Lyra was still having trouble breathing. It felt as if her lungs were wrapped in medical gauze. She leaned back against the garage, which was made of cinder block and very cool, and closed her eyes. The space was full of spiderwebs and wet leaves. It smelled like decay. What was the point, anyway? How long did she really have?

Half of her wanted simply to walk out into the road and wait for their pursuers to find her. Where would they take her? She would be reunited with the rest of the replicas, she was sure. Or maybe she would be killed and her body disposed of. Maybe they were erasing the experiment, slowly eradicating all indications that Haven had ever existed. But it would be easier. So much easier.

'You can't give up now,' Caelum said. 'Lyra. Listen to me.' He put a hand on her cheek and she opened her eyes. His thumb moved along the ridge of her cheekbone, as it had last night. His lips were very close. His eyes were dark and long-lashed. Beautiful. 'You named me. That means I'm yours, doesn't it? I'm yours and you're mine.'

'I'm scared,' Lyra said. And she was – scared of the running, scared of what would happen to them, but scared, too, of how close he was standing, of how her body changed when he touched her and became fluid-feeling, as if something hard deep inside of her were softening. She knew that there were electrical currents in the body and that was what she was reminded of now, of currents flowing between them, of thousands of lights.

'I'm scared too,' he said. He leaned forward and touched his forehead to hers. And still her body called out for something, something more and deeper and closer, but she didn't know what. She wished them out of the bodies that divided them. She thought of the word *love*, and wondered whether this, this feeling of never being able to get close enough, was it. She had never been taught. But she thought so.

'I love you,' she said. The words felt strange, foreign to her, like a new food. But not unpleasant.

'I love you,' Caelum repeated back to her, and smiled. She could tell the words were just as surprising to him. He said them again. 'I love you.'

Inside her chest, a door opened, and she found she was at last breathing easily, and now had the strength to go on.

They made it back into town without seeing the sedan again, but they were standing at the first bus stop they could find, debating where to go next, when Lyra spotted the man from the house in a parking lot across the road, passing between the businesses, delis, and retail shops that were clustered together, like beads someone had strung along the same necklace. She took Caelum's hand and they hurried to the most crowded place they could find: a dim restaurant called the Blue Gator, separated from the road by a scrub of sad little trees. Dozens of men were crowded around a counter, drinking and watching sports, occasionally letting out a cheer or a groan in unison. Lyra and Caelum moved toward the back of the restaurant, past old wood tables filled with kids squabbling over plates of french fries and couples drinking and staring dull-eyed at the TVs. A hallway led back toward the kitchen. A girl with a haircut almost like Lyra's was standing beneath a sign that indicated a restroom, her fingers skating over the screen of her phone, her chin prominent in the blue light cast by its glow. Lyra had an idea.

She took Jake Witz's phone from her pocket.

'Hello.' Lyra held out the phone. The girl's eyes jumped from her screen to Lyra to Caelum. 'Can you please help?'

'Help with what?' the girl said. She didn't sound mean, but she didn't sound exactly friendly, either. Caelum kept turning around to look at the door, to make sure they hadn't been followed, and the girl ignored Lyra to watch him.

'We need to find Gemma,' Lyra said. 'In the phone,' she added impatiently, and finally the short-haired girl dragged her eyes from Caelum to look at her. 'We need to find Gemma in the phone. We don't know how.'

The girl snorted. She had a metal ring in her nose. 'Are you serious?' When Lyra didn't answer, she rolled her eyes and took the phone. She made several quick movements with her fingers and then passed the phone back to Lyra. 'You should really keep that thing locked, you know. Do I get a prize now?'

Lyra's heart leapt. She pressed the phone to her ear but heard nothing but silence. She shook her head. 'It's not *working*.'

'Jesus. Where do you *come* from? The 1800s?' The girl snatched the phone back, made another quick adjustment, and then jammed it to Lyra's ear. 'Happy now?'

The phone was ringing. Lyra held her breath. She counted one ring, two rings, three. How long would it ring, she wondered? But then there was a nearly inaudible click.

'Jake?' Gemma's voice sounded so close Lyra nearly jerked the phone away in surprise. 'Is that you?'

Lyra turned away, so the short-haired girl, who was still watching her suspiciously, wouldn't be able to hear. 'It's not Jake,' she said. 'Jake is dead. And we need your help.'

SIXTEEN

GEMMA AND A BLOND-HAIRED BOY named Pete arrived just as a man in an apron was badgering Lyra and Caelum to order something or leave. Lyra was afraid to go outside. She thought it likely that the people who'd been in Jake's house were still out there, walking the streets, waiting for them. So when Gemma came through the crowd — her eyes big and worried in that pretty moon-face, the face that had so recently belonged to Cassiopeia — she felt a wash of relief so strong she nearly began to cry. They were safe.

'It's all right. They're with us, and we're leaving,' Gemma said, and the man in his apron scurried away. 'Are you okay?' she asked, and Lyra nodded. She felt as if a hand had reached down and picked her up. And again, a memory came to her of warmth and closeness, an impression of one of the birthers rocking her, singing in her ear.

But she knew it must be made up. The birthers didn't hold the human models they made. They came and were kept in the darkness of the barracks, and were sent away in darkness, too, after receiving their pay.

The birthers weren't male, either. But in her memory, or her imagination, or her fantasy, she felt the tickle of a beard on her forehead, and clear gray eyes, and a man's hands, scarred across the knuckles, touching her face.

Caelum always kept close to her now. Even in the car he sat only inches away from Lyra, with one hand pressed to hers. She understood that they were bound together, and she thought of their lives and their fates like a double-stranded helix, wound around each other, webbed with meaning. And she felt that next to him she could face anything, even a slow death, even the world that kept unfolding into new highways and more people and a greater horizon.

In the car, Lyra told Gemma about going to track down Emily Huang and discovering she was dead.

'I could have told you that,' Gemma said, and Lyra heard the criticism in her voice: *If you hadn't run*. She was getting better at sorting out tones and moods.

She described how they had found the card with Jake's address and determined to go and find him. She told Gemma about the unlocked screen door and finding him in the bedroom with a crust of dried blood on his lips.

'They must have come for him right after we left,' Gemma whispered to the boy, Pete. 'God. I might throw up.'

'It's not your fault,' he said, and reached out to place a hand on her thigh. Lyra saw this and wondered if Gemma and Pete were bound in the same way she was to Caelum.

'Both of them strung up, made to look like suicides,' Gemma said, and turned away to cough. There had been a fire, she had told them, but Lyra would have known anyway. The whole car smelled like smoke. 'Must be the military's little specialty.'

'Less suspicious, maybe, than a gun,' Pete said.

She told them about the man and woman who'd shown up only a few minutes later to finish the job of staging a suicide, and how she'd nearly been caught and had to hide behind the sofa.

'Holy shit,' Pete said, and this time it was Gemma who reached over to squeeze *his* leg.

'I took his computer,' Lyra said.

Gemma turned around in her seat. 'You what?'

'I don't know why.' Lyra was still ashamed that they'd stolen Jake's cell phone and left in the middle of the night. She didn't want Gemma to hate her. 'I thought it might be useful, so I took it.'

Gemma blinked. If Lyra squinted, she could pretend

she was looking at Cassiopeia instead – a healthy Cassiopeia, a Cassiopeia with soft brown hair and a quick smile. She could have been number 11.

'That's brilliant,' Gemma said. 'You're a genius.'

Caelum spoke up too, to explain why they had run, and Gemma seemed to understand. Lyra was intensely relieved: she wondered whether in some strange way, some mystery of biology, she and Gemma got along for the same reason she had always liked Cassiopeia.

'And I almost forgot.' She took the backpack wedged at Caelum's feet and removed the papers and photos she'd found hidden behind the picture frames at Sheri's house. 'Before she died, Nurse Em gave three pieces of art to her next-door neighbor. I found these hidden in the backing.'

Gemma held the pages in her hands carefully, as if they were insect wings. She stared for a long time at the list of names that Lyra hadn't been able to make sense of. 'Can I keep these?' she asked.

'Okay.' Lyra had been looking forward to rebuilding her collection of reading materials, using these pages as a start to her new library. But she knew they might be important – they must be, if Nurse Em had wanted them to stay hidden.

'I'll give them back, I promise,' Gemma said, as if she knew what Lyra was thinking. Gemma seemed to have that uncanny ability. Lyra wondered whether Gemma was special, or whether she was simply the first person to care what Lyra thought and felt. Gemma folded the pages carefully and tucked them inside a pocket. Lyra was sorry to see them go. 'Look,' Gemma said. 'There's something I need to tell you. Something about your past.'

The car jerked. Pete had barely swerved to avoid an object in the road, some kind of animal, Lyra thought, although they were past it too quickly for her to make out what it was.

'What?' she said. 'What is it?' She was suddenly afraid but couldn't say why. She thought she could feel Caelum's pulse beating through her palm. She thought it began to beat faster.

Gemma was squinting as if trying to see through a hard light. 'You weren't actually made at Haven.'

A burst of white behind Lyra's eyes – a sure sign of a bad headache to come. *Side effects. Symptoms.* She pictured those hands again, the scar across the knuckles, the tickle of a beard on her forehead. Imagination. Fantasy.

'What do you mean?' It was Caelum who spoke. 'Where was she made?'

'Nowhere,' Gemma said, and Lyra heard the word as if it was coming to her through water. As if she was drowning. *Nowhere.* A terrible, lonely word. 'This list is of kids who got taken from their families and brought to Haven, at a time the institute couldn't afford to keep making human models. The third name, Brandy-Nicole Harliss, is your birth name. Your *real* name. That's the name your parents gave you.'

Next to her, Caelum twitched. Lyra's lungs didn't feel like they were working. She could hardly breathe. 'My . . .' She couldn't say the word *parents*. It didn't make sense. She thought of the birthers in the barracks and the new replicas sleeping in their pretty little incubators in Postnatal. That was her world. That was where she'd come from.

'You have parents,' Gemma said gently, as if she was delivering bad news. And it *was* bad news. It was unimaginable, horrific. Lyra had wondered sometimes about what it would be like to have Dr. O'Donnell as a mother, what it would be like to have parents, generally, but never had she truly thought about being a person, natural-born, exploded into being by chance. One of *them*. 'Well, you have a father. He's been looking for you all this time. He's loved you all this time.'

That word, *love*. It shocked her. It hit her like a blade in the chest and she cried out, feeling the pain of it, the raw unexpectedness, as if an old wound had opened. Although she had dreamed when she was little about going home with one of the nurses – although she'd even, secretly, imagined Dr. O'Donnell returning for her one day, taking Lyra in a lemon-scented hug – these were fantasies, and even in her fantasies home looked much like Haven, with white walls and high lights and the soothing sounds of rubber soles on linoleum.

She didn't want love, not from a stranger, not from a *father.* She was a replica.

Caelum took his hand from hers. He turned back toward the window.

No, she wanted to say. She felt somehow dirty. *It isn't true. It can't be.* But she was paralyzed, suffocating under the weight of what Gemma had told her. She couldn't move to touch Caelum's arm, to tell him it was all right. She couldn't ask him to forgive her.

He didn't look at her at all after that.

SEVENTEEN

SHE DIDN'T WANT A FATHER.

She had never even known what a father did, had never completely understood why fathers were necessary. When she tried to imagine one now she thought instead of God, of his dark beard and narrow eyes, of the way he always seemed to be sneering, even when he smiled. She thought of Werner, whose fingers were yellowed and smelled like smoke; or of Nurse Wanna Bet, a male, pinching her skin before inserting the syringes, or fiddling with IV bags, or poking her stomach for signs of distention.

And yet, alongside these ideas was her impression – her memory? – of that plastic cup, of hands rocking her to sleep and the tickle of a beard.

Caelum didn't speak again until they stopped for the night, just outside of a place called Savannah. Lyra was both relieved and disappointed to learn they wouldn't be going on. She was dreading meeting her father, whoever he was, but also desperate to get it over with, and had assumed Gemma would take her straight back to him. Now she would have to live instead with her fantasy of him, his face transforming into the face of various Haven doctors and nurses, into the soldiers on the marshes with their helmets and guns, into the hard look of the men who came on unmarked barges to load the body when a replica had died: these were the only men she had ever known.

They stopped at an enormous parking lot full of other vehicles, concealed from the highway beneath a heavy line of plane trees and shaded by woods on all sides. Gemma told her that these camps existed across the country for people traveling by camper van and RV – two words Lyra didn't know, although she assumed they referred to the type of cars parked in the lot, which looked as though they'd been inflated to four times normal size – and once again she was struck by just how many people there must be in the world, enough so that even the ones traveling between towns had their own little network of places to stop for the night. It made her sad. She wondered whether she would ever feel she had a place in this world.

All she knew was that if she had a place, it must be with Caelum.

'I'll be back,' Caelum said when they got out of the

231

GEMMA

car – the first words he had spoken in hours.

'I'll come with you,' Lyra said quickly. But she found that walking next to him, she couldn't find words to say what she wanted to say. It was as if a wall had come down between them. She felt as if he was a stranger again, as if he was the boy she'd met out on the marshes. Even his face looked different – harder, more angular.

At one end of the camp was a whitewashed building with separate bathrooms for men and women, and shower stalls that could be accessed by putting coins in a slot in the lockbox on the doors. Lyra found she did after all want a shower. She wished she could wash off the past few hours: the dizzying reality that somewhere out there were people who'd birthed her, the memory of Jake Witz's face, bloated and terrible, and the smell of blood and sick that still seemed to hang to her clothes. How did she even know Gemma was telling her the truth? But she trusted Gemma instinctively, no matter what Caelum had originally feared, and when Gemma offered her coins to work the door, she accepted.

The shower was slick with soap scum and reminded her of the bright tiles of Haven and all the replicas showering in groups, herded under the showers in three-minute bursts. She missed that. She missed the order, the routine, the nurses telling her where to go and when. But at the same time the Lyra who was content to float through the days, who lay down on the paper-covered medical beds and let Squeezeme and Thermoscan do their work, who thought of them as friends, even, felt impossibly foreign. She couldn't remember being that girl.

She had no towel, so when she got dressed again, her hair, still wet, dampened her shoulders and her shirt. But she felt better, cleaner. A father. She experimented with holding the idea for two, three seconds at a time now without shame. She brushed up next to it, got close, sniffed around it like an animal exploring something new. What would it be like to have a father? What did a father actually *do*? She had no idea.

She came outside into a night loud with distant laughter and the sound of tree frogs. She didn't see Caelum. She took a turn of the building and found him in the back, hurling rocks into the growth where the dirt clearing petered out into cypress and shade trees.

'Caelum?' He didn't turn around and, thinking he hadn't heard, she took another step forward. 'Caelum?'

'Don't call me that.' He turned to face her, his face caught in the flare of the floodlights, and her stomach went hollow. He looked as if he hated her. 'That's not my name.' This time he directed a volley of rocks at the restrooms, so they pinged against the stucco walls and the sign pointing the way to the showers. 'I'm seventy-two. I'm a replica. A human model. Only humans have names.'

Then she knew that what she'd been afraid of was true. He hated her for what she was, or for what she wasn't.

'You're wrong,' Lyra said. She felt as if she were being squeezed between two giant plates, as if the whole world had narrowed to this moment. 'That isn't what makes the difference.'

'Oh yeah? You would know, I guess.' He looked away. 'I thought we were the same, but we're not. We're different. *You're* different.'

'So what?' Lyra took a step closer to him. They were separated by less than a foot, but he might have been on the other side of the world. She felt reckless, desperate, the same way she'd felt running after Haven had exploded. He turned back to her, frowning. 'So we're different. Who cares? We chose to escape together. We chose to stay together. We chose each other, didn't we?' *I gave you a name,* she almost said, but the memory of that night, and lying so close to him, while the darkness stirred around his body, made her throat constrict. 'That's what makes the difference. Getting to choose, and what you choose.' She took a breath. 'I choose you.'

'How can you?' His voice was raw. 'You know what I am. I don't belong anywhere.'

'You belong with me.' When she said it out loud, she knew it was true. 'Please.' She'd never had to ask for anything, because she'd never had reason to. But this woke

inside of her – the asking and the need, the feeling that if
he didn't say yes, she wouldn't be able to go on.

'Please,' she repeated, because she could say nothing
else. But at the same time she took a step toward him and
put a hand on his chest, above his heart, because there was
always that to return to, always the truth of its rhythm
and the fact that every person, no matter how they were
formed or where, had a heart that worked the same way.

They were inches apart. His skin was hot. And though
she could feel him, touch him, *know* his separateness, in
that moment she also learned something totally new –
that it was possible by touching someone else to dissolve
all the space between them.

'I am no one,' he said. In his eyes she was reflected in
duplicate. 'I was made to be no one.'

'You're someone to me,' she said. 'You're everything.'

He took her face in his hands and kissed her. They had
never learned how to kiss, either of them. But somehow
he knew. She did, too. It was beyond instinct. It was joy.

They were clumsy, still. They stumbled and then she
was against the wall. She pulled herself into him and
found to her amazement that her body knew more than
how to ache or shiver or exhaust itself. It knew how to
sing.

They barely touched except with their mouths, the
way they explored together *teeth tongue lips*, the way they

shivered with the joy of discovery. They were born for the first time in their bodies. They were born together. They came together into the world as everyone should – frightened, uncertain, amazed, grateful.

And for them the world was born, too, in all its complexity and strange glory. They had a place in it, at last, and so at last it became theirs to share. No matter what happened, no matter what trouble came, Lyra knew they would face it together, as they were then: turned human by joy, by a belonging that felt just like freedom.